Learnin' the Ropes

"Okay, you tough-talkin' hick-town lawman!" a man yelled from the cracked-open door of the schoolhouse. "This is Pierce Starky and your time's up. So you wanna ask the folks out there if they got any preference to which of the small fry gets it first?"

"Kill any of them you like. Any child or the teacher," the sheriff yelled. A rumble of alarmed talk from the body of watchers threatened to drown out what the lawman was saying. So he raised his voice, matching the composed tone of Starky, to drive his fellow citizens back into silence. "But know this, you men! You shoot one of your hostages, you might just as well shoot all of them! We can only string you up once!"

Other titles in the **EDGE** series from Pinnacle Books

#48

EDGE

SCHOOL FOR SLAUGHTER

►BY◄

George G. Gilman

PINNACLE BOOKS NEW YORK

This novel is a work of fiction. Names, characters, places, and incidents are either the product of the author's imagination or are used fictitiously. Any resemblance to actual events or places or persons, living or dead, is entirely coincidental.

EDGE #48: SCHOOL FOR SLAUGHTER

Copyright © 1985 by George G. Gilman

A Pinnacle Books edition, published by special arrangement with New English Library.

Pinnacle edition/February 1985

ISBN: 0-523-42267-9

Printed in the United States of America

PINNACLE BOOKS, INC.
1430 Broadway
New York, New York 10018

9 8 7 6 5 4 3 2 1

For H.S.
I hope more and better things
come to you who waited so long!

Chapter One

IT LOOKED and smelled like rain as Sheriff Richard J. Morrow left his office on Main Street across from the River Road spur and began his regular midafternoon patrol through Loganville, Kansas. Heavy rain too, the man with the five-pointed silver star pinned to the left side of his vest estimated after a frowning glance at the low, discolored sky as he took a deep breath of the unseasonable chill air. The kind of rain that might suggest heaven was angry at the sins of the world rather than was weeping for the sad state it was in, the lawman reflected morosely as he varied the usually unvarying route of his regular patrol. He moved across the broad width of Main, which ran arrow straight east to west, passed the Cottonwood Saloon on the corner and the South Wind Hotel that faced it, and headed northeast along the equally straight but much narrower River Road toward his small house.

Rich Morrow was by nature a proud man who never looked more proud of himself than when he was striding through the town in which he had been the peace officer for so long. He was a tall, lean, upright-of-stature man, nearer to sixty than fifty but not prepared to admit to this, and for the most part able to sustain the harmless lie. For his black hair was thick and ungrayed, his blue eyes were clear and farsighted, and his bronzed complexion was less cut with lines than many men a lot younger.

He was dressed Western-style in a check shirt of subdued red and black, black buckskin vest, denim pants of a slightly lighter hue, and a kerchief of the same color. His clothing went regularly to be laundered by the town's washwoman. He kept his boots highly polished himself and likewise attended to his cream-colored Stetson and black gun belt and holster. There was a Walker Colt in the holster and a bullet in every loop of the belt, and the revolver, ammunition, and the metal studs that decorated the band of his hat gleamed with the same sheen of painstaking care as the badge of Morrow's office.

His single-story four-room clapboard house was third in a line of ten homes of varying sizes and styles that stretched out along the northwest side of River Road between the hotel and the plank bridge that spanned the fifteen-foot width of Sunflower Creek. He was inside for just a few seconds; during that time the first raindrops of an impending storm spattered down on Loganville and the vast, sparsely populated countryside that rolled away across the Great Plains in every direction from town. As he closed the door of his house and moved down the cement walk between the rectangles of neatly cut turf, Morrow nodded in self-satisfaction at his wisdom in writing home for the yellow slicker that now draped him from shoulder to knee. As he reached the street the initial gust of what could develop into a strong blow buffeted his hat and tugged at the loose-fitting slicker, and he took more than usual care to ensure that the latch on the gate in the newly repainted picket fence that bounded his property was securely fastened. Then, as he strolled up River Road in the direction of the creek he took the trouble to glance at other people's gateways in addition to making the routine survey of their properties as a whole.

In the manner he moved along the thoroughfare and ran his watchful gaze over the flanking houses, there was an unconscious attitude of possessiveness about the lawman. This attitude was not in any way diminished when he inclined his head or exchanged a laconic greeting with those men or women who acknowledged his passing; in fact, it was heightened by the presence of people, for, as he reminded himself, it was far more important to safeguard people than property.

Mrs. Grace Eden, whose husband was the town butcher, was hurrying to bring in the wash from the line in her backyard when she waved to Morrow. Diagonally across from the Eden house, Luke Farris ignored the rain and the entreaties of his wife as he worked at his usual sluggish pace to hang a new front door in the frame. It was a long overdue repair to the two-story house that was badly neglected in many other respects. But as Loganville's only skilled carpenter, Farris resented the need to undertake such unpaid chores de-

3

manded by his long-suffering wife. Today, he would have been happy to interrupt his current job and stand in the now steadily falling rain and talk with Morrow.

"Told Harriet first thing this morning it was gonna rain, Rich, and it was no day to start on outside work."

"There you go, Luke." The lawman ignored what the disgruntled carpenter was saying and, by not pausing in his measured progress over the rain-softened surface of the street, caused Farris to sigh into silence.

Then, as Morrow nodded in the direction of Ivy Rankinn, the wife of the mortician, as she hastily closed the windows of the next-door house, he was not unaware of the grateful look Harriet Farris directed toward him. There was no one at home in the last house on his left, for Sam Dyer was a widower and would be at work in his forge and little Emily was still in school. The Dyer gate was swinging and creaking in the strengthening wind and the lawman was pleased to be able to fasten the latch. He was even more pleased when he realized this simple act of neighborliness had been noticed.

"Obliged to you, Sheriff!" Olive Carlin called from the open doorway of the house directly across the street, a two-room shack where her husband, who was the Loganville barber, hung his hat and rested his carcass when he was not working in his shop or drinking in the Cottonwood. "Was startin' to make a racket that'd give a body a headache! And I didn't wanna get soaked to the skin goin' over there myself to shut it up! Get soaked and get my nose filled with the stink of them hogs and hens of old man Kyne's now the wind's blowin' right from his place to Nathan's and mine!"

"You're welcome, ma'am," Morrow answered as he went on by her house, and he took no umbrage at the violence with which she slammed the door. For Olive Carlin had taken to the bottle herself in recent months, and when she was drunk, her normal placidity was overpowered by a latent streak of perversity. But nobody who knew her well and was aware of her usual timid nature when sober ever took offense at her harsh tongue and rash actions when she was drunk.

The wind was driving the rain with stinging force into the sheriff's grim set face and he took the precaution of tightening the chin cord of his hat as he neared the end of his patrol out along River Road. Borne on the wind, which was blowing north and northeast, was the pungent smell from Ira Kyne's pig and chicken farm of which Mrs. Carlin had complained. But the stink of the place that was out beside the open trail on the other side of the plank bridge could be a whole lot worse on a hot summer day. Few citizens of Loganville ever griped seriously about Ira Kyne's noisome livestock, though, because few of the townspeople did not relish the cured bacon the old man supplied through Ralph Eden's meat market and the fresh eggs that were retailed at the Wades's grocery store.

The town-limits marker was on this side of the bridge over the creek that continued to run gently, not yet swollen with rain water rushing north to the Arkansas River. But Rich Morrow looked upon the Kyne place and the one-room shack of Betsy Blake—even farther out along the other side of the trail—as being part of "his" town, and so he cracked his eyes against the assault of the wind-driven raindrops and raked his gaze over the barb-wire-fenced Kyne property and the more distant tin-roofed and timber-walled home of the black washwoman. Then, satisfied that all was as it should be in his jurisdiction beyond the plank bridge, he stepped off the road and turned into the pathway that curved through the stand of cottonwoods at the base of a grassy knoll on the creek bank.

Although he was constantly host to a proprietary feeling toward Loganville, there were times when for no clear-cut reason he felt this unfounded sense of ownership more strongly than usual. Now was just such an occasion, which was why he consciously elected to exclude the Meadowlark Ranch from any consideration as he turned his back on River Road to head through the stand of timber to the place where the trail from Wichita became the eastern end of Main Street. For the ranch, the property line of which crossed the northeast trail two miles beyond the Loganville town limit, was owned by Spiro Logan. And when Rich Morrow was in the frame of mind he was currently in this wet and windswept, chill and darkened afternoon, he came close to experiencing a powerful hatred of Spiro Logan and everything the rancher stood for—and the lawman was ashamed of harboring such a groundless but deep-seated emotion.

Had he not been in such a mood, he might well have spent a few more moments at the plank bridge, peering into the angling rain. And he would certainly have seen the trio of riders who galloped their mounts up out of a hollow through which the trail dipped—a sight that would have caused him to remain at the end of River Road for long enough to see if the three horsemen were strangers to Loganville. But the cottonwoods and then the more solid bulk of the knoll came between Morrow and the riders. And next the hiss of teeming rain and the swish of the wind in high foliage masked the thud of hooves on the muddied trail and the brief, much louder drumming of the hard-ridden horses galloping over the bridge.

The pathway emerged into the open at the side fence of the old and now unused stockyards, directly opposite the Kansas Corral with Sam Dyer's forge in one front corner. The smoke from the blacksmith's roaring fire was strong in the sodden air in this part of town, and Morrow could hear Dyer hammering a piece of metal on his anvil in back of the double doors that were closed against the weather. A half-dozen horses were restlessly pacing back and forth or circling one way and then another within the corral's timber fencing. And they whinnied, tossed their heads, and quivered the flesh of their flanks. Familiar as they were with the smells and sounds of the forge, it had to be some other aspect of their surroundings that was disturbing the animals—and when a distant flash of sheet lightning lit up the black sky, Morrow realized the horses had sensed that the storm was going to bring more than just rain and wind.

The lightning had left the sky for several seconds before the first sound of rolling thunder reached across the Great Plains to be heard in Loganville. The horses stood stock still in the churned-up mud of the corral, their ears pricked to listen intently until the final trace of thunder disappeared. Then they started to circle and pace and toss their heads and swing their tails again, unwilling and perhaps unable to remain in stoic expectation of the next flash and rumble that they knew would come.

Morrow was about to cross Main Street and go into the forge to warn Sam Dyer about the horses in the corral being spooked. But Drew Grogan came hobbling out of the stage-line depot across the alley from the forge, with young Ansel Twist close behind.

"Looks set in for a real mean one, Rich!" the lame Grogan yelled. "And that there team in the corral knows it surer than any man can see it!"

The skinny and lithe youngster ran on ahead and vaulted the three-bar fence beyond the forge with athletic ease as Grogan held back to hammer with his walking cane on one of Sam Dyer's doors.

"You need a hand, Drew?" Morrow called.

"Us three'll manage! Best you go warn folks to stow under cover anythin' that ain't nailed down."

This is what the lawman had in mind to do, even thought he had more confidence in the commonsense of his fellow citizens than did the depot manager. But maybe someone—and Nathan Carlin was not the only likely candidate—had spent too much time drinking too much liquor in the Cottonwood and needed to be woken up to the danger. And so, thinking only of the welfare and safety of the people of Loganville, Rich Morrow spared not a single glance out along the trail that stretched due east toward Wichita, forty-some miles away beyond sparsely populated prairie. Thus he failed to glimpse the lone horseman who had ridden unhurriedly into sight out of the teeming rain just as the storm-spooked animals in the Kansas Corral had captured the sheriff's attention.

Morrow had also not seen, at a second opportunity, the trio of riders who rode into Loganville on River Road—was engaged in the exchange with Drew Grogan when the three men, walking their horses now, moved across the intersection with Main and headed west. As the sheriff began to move in the same direction with longer strides than before, there was too much activity along the street for any aspect of the scene to stand out from the whole—particularly with the wind-driven rain that was the cause of the sudden bustle.

Saddle horses, horses and wagons, and people on foot hurried this way and that as they realized the darkened sky had brought the violent weather it promised from the start, and business was speedily concluded or abruptly curtailed by those who suddenly had more pressing missions elsewhere in Loganville. Sheet lightning blazed across the almost nightlike sky with increasing brilliance and frequency and each successive roll of thunder was louder. The wind gusted more forcefully and rain pelted at anything solid with a seemingly destructive intent.

When the dazzling brightness of the lightning was not hurling intense white light and dense black shadows through the town, the frail glow of lamplit windows angled irregular wedges of yellow over the scene of frenetic activity. Once the citizens of Loganville realized just what kind of storm was going to be unleashed upon them, they quickly calmed down. So that before Rich Morrow had taken more than twenty or thirty paces toward the midtown area, the excitement was confined to the children who had been let out of school just before the first flash of lightning and roll of thunder. The lawman noted with a glow of pride that spread an uncharacteristic smile across his rugged face that only a few of the very youngest students were afraid of the ferocity of the storm. The rest of Loganville's small fry seemed to be enjoying the weather, maybe because it had caused Arlene Heller to release them from the classroom some thirty minutes ahead of the usual time.

Morrow was beyond the old stockyards and corral and stage-line depot now, his alert survey of the town and its citizens less hampered by the driving rain which was no longer needling into his face. To his right was a line of houses more crowded together and smaller than most of those on River Road. They were the only properties in town still owned by the man for whose family Loganville was named and were rented to those men with families who worked at the Meadowlark Ranch. The women with the youngest children bustled along the ever-muddier street to bring them home while others peered anxiously from their open doorways into the thronging traffic between this section of Main Street and the schoolhouse.

Anxious faces lit with relief as children were seen to be hurrying home. Others showed varying degrees of parental displeasure when more youngsters were spotted fooling around in the rain and mud. A few remained set in worried frowns as the curtain of rain and the scramble to get clear of it continued to hide the stragglers.

"I'll light fires under their rears, Mrs. Sullivan, Mrs. Bass, Mrs. Nightingale!" the sheriff called with a reassuring grin as he strode purposefully down the center of the street. Then he had to interrupt himself as a crackle of thunder sounded hard on the heels of a flash of lightning before he added: "Don't any of you good ladies worry none! I'll see to it they all get home and outta this directly!"

Those women concerned for the safety of their children and those who shared in their neighbors' anxiety were momentarily placated by Rich Morrow's confident attitude, and many were able to raise smiles of gratitude for the Loganville lawman who had earned the respect of the entire town.

Across the street from the Spiro Logan–owned houses, the telegraph office, Abner Coburn's Livery, the building where Byron Pardo tended sick animals and pulled human teeth, and Luke Farris's lumber store were all secured against the ravaging storm. Morrow grinned complacently and nodded. But then, as he neared the point where he had begun the swing through the eastern side of town, his demeanor underwent a sudden change.

The movement of horses and wagons had caused him to angle off the center of the street and he had gone to the south side, across from the Main frontage of the Cottonwood Saloon and toward his law office and adjacent jailhouse. All the time he good-naturedly berated the dawdling children to get home to their worried mothers and also responded cheerfully to the men and women who called out sardonic comments about the springtime weather. But when Gideon Doyle taunted, "I maybe ain't free as no bird, Mr. Lawman, but I sure is real nice and dry in here!"—Morrow came to an angry halt alongside the only window in the brick jailhouse that looked out on to the street. He scowled back

11

at the black man whose grinning face was pressed against the bars and whose hands were fisted around two of them, unable to catch hold of a retort while he adjusted to the unexpected change of mood.

Then he rasped between clenched teeth, "Dry inside and out, swillbelly. Until you start getting the sweats from being so long without the Cottonwood rotgut, uh?" He shifted his angry eyes to the two-story saloon across the now less crowded, much muddier street. Then he returned his gaze to the Negro in the cell and cruelly lit tiny fires in his eyes as he said to the only citizen of Loganville who held him in low regard: "Won't be long now, I figure. Won't be long, either, before I see this town's battened down against the storm. And then I think maybe I'll step over to the Cottonwood myself. Have me a few snorts of Joe Synder's best sipping bourbon. Sit at my favorite table while I'm partaking of that. Or maybe sit out on the stoop in one of the rockers, if the wind lets up."

He looked pointedly across the street again and the no longer grinning Doyle stared sourly in the same direction. There was a trace of the former grin back on the lawman's face when he returned his gaze to the discomforted Negro. But it was immediately displaced by another scowl when the man in the cell snarled through the bars: "If what I seen while you been struttin' throught this tank town means what I think it means, Mr. Lawman, you ain't gonna have no time for takin' no drinks! Fast or sippin' style!"

"What's that supposed to mean, swillbelly?" Morrow countered, and immediately regretted paying heed to what Doyle had said. He looked hurriedly around to check that none of the town's solid citizens had over-heard him, then pushed his face close to the bars of the cell window to rasp at the black man who backed away: "Never mind, swillbelly! Sprawl your stinking body out on the cot again and dream up some more crazy notions! And wail all you like about not having your ever-loving woman in there with you. With the weather the way it is you won't disturb anybody!"

It was as if the storm were prompted to emphasize Morrow's point. For the wind abruptly drove more powerfully across the intersection of Main Street and River Road, driving the rain with far noisier force against everything solid and growling through gaps. An instant later a violent creak of thunder seemed to rock the ground upon which the town was built as the bright-est flash of lightning yet flared with dazzling intensity through the torrent.

"You'll see what I mean, you hard-nosed sonofa-bitch!" Gideon Doyle shrieked as he whirled from the window and hurled himself down on the straw mattress that covered the narrow cot, scowling his hatred for the lawman up at the ceiling. "Where that mean-as-a-rattlesnake Animal is, you can be sure that trouble ain't never far behind him!"

Rich Morrow did not hear either the insult or the cryptic comment yelled by the Negro, for he was tempo-rarily deafened by the thunder; he was turning away from the cell window at the same time as Doyle flung himself back from it to sprawl on the cot.

In the brightness of the lightning flash, the midtown intersection was seen to be almost deserted—except for the lawman out front of the jailhouse, a lone rider who was slowly moving into town from the east between the Kansas Corral and the old stockyards, three travel-weary saddle horses hitched to a rail outside one of the business premises on the south side of the western stretch of Main, and ten-year-old Carrie Blair, who sat in the mud with her hands clasped in her blond hair and her skinny frame shaking with sobs.

Then, in the aftermath of the brilliant glare that had seemed to give the entire town an incandescent glow, there were just the glimmering wedges of lamplight to hold back the darkness of the afternoon. But this was suffi-cient for the lawman to see that Carrie Blair had need to fear more than what her child's imagination had con-jured up out of the sights and sounds of the electric storm.

For the horses tethered to the rail along the street were also terrified by what they could not understand and reared and plunged, hooves flailing, against the restraints of the reins hitched to the rail. The lawman had taken just a few paces toward the hysterical little girl when the three spooked horses succeeded in snap-ping the rail. Two of the freed animals wheeled to gallop westward while the third reared and lunged in the opposite direction.

Rich Morrow spurted forward into a run of his own then, mud splashing up from under his pumping feet, his gaze raking between the bolting horse and the sob-bing child. As his left hand tugged at his slicker so that his right could reach beneath and draw the Walker Colt, his throat constricted with self-doubt for the first time he could recall in many years. He wondered if, should there be no other way to save little Carrie Blair, he would be able to drop the fear-crazed horse with the handgun.

He dragged the revolver from the holster just as the child sensed the danger she was in. Her eyes, big and round and bulging, saw the man with the gun staggering through the storm toward her. She vented a shrill scream, and as Morrow swung his gaze from the galloping horse to the girl his leading foot hooked under a short plank of timber that had been dislodged from a fast-rolling wagon and been half buried in the churned-up mud of the intersection.

A groan of dismay ripped from between his clenched teeth as he pitched headlong into the ooze, and then cried in alarm when the jolt of the tumble squeezed his finger hard to the trigger of the just-cocked gun.

The bullet spattered into the mud. Carrie Blair half rose and then seemed to be rooted to where she stood, her hands still clasped at the top of her head. The bolting horse kept on coming. The Loganville sheriff unglued himself from the sucking surface of the intersection and began to stagger forward again while he was still in a crouch. The horse veered to the side and raced in back of Morrow, close enough for the pumping hooves to spray more mud over the lawman.

Morrow yelled: "It's all right, Carrie! It's me, Carrie! Uncle Rich, honey! Let's go!"

He scooped her up in his left arm. His touch unfroze her and she kicked and scratched at him. But he held on to the struggling form tenaciously as he ran faster up the less mired surface of River Road. He had abandoned efforts to placate her and was experiencing deep anger. Not at Carrie, though. His tight-lipped fury was directed at Patsy Blair, who would certainly not be giving anyone a piano or violin lesson in these circumstances but whose mind—and body?—must surely be engaged in a more diverting pursuit for her not to be alive to what was happening outside the confines of her neat little house.

The only man now out in the rain on the entire length of Main Street eased his grip on the half-drawn Winchester and the rifle slid fully back into the boot. Then the hand that had let go of the repeater moved forward to commence a gentle stroking action along the neck of his mount—which he continued until the runaway horse had headed out along the east trail.

The two other spooked animals were already long gone off into the country to the west of Loganville.

A few moments earlier, in the bank behind the rail to which the horses had been hitched, the three men who had ridden them into town drew and aimed their revolvers at Leroy Albertson, Faith Kruger, and Adele Vicary. And grinned cheerfully at the middle-aged banker and his two elderly assistants. All six people in the softly lit room were oblivious to the sounds of the storm beyond the firmly closed door.

"Mr. Albertson?" the redheaded Faith Kruger gasped, a hand to her mouth.

"Leroy?" the second, long-past-her-prime spinster pleaded, eyeglasses glinting.

"Easy, gentlemen," the round-faced and usually ruddy-complected banker urged, the fear in his throat forcing his voice to the level of a harsh whisper.

"Sure as shit is easy," the gun-toting stranger in the center growled through his grinning teeth.

"Easy's how we figure to take it," the one with the mustache added in the same composed manner.

The third, the ugliest of the men, triggered the first shot. In the barrage of bullets that this signaled, he snarled amid his own raucous laughter: "And we're takin' ever last friggin' cent, you hicks!"

Chapter Two

THE BANK that Leroy Albertson managed with his two spinster assistants in Loganville was just a minor branch office of the Kansas Mutual Trust Corporation in Wichita. It never carried large amounts of cash unless for a specific purpose, and for such transactions the money was seldom on the premises for more than a few hours. Thus, the one-room single-story gray stone building was not designed to withstand a holdup—particularly such a cold-blooded brutal assault as was launched upon it that storm-darkened springtime afternoon.

The gunmen stood on one side of the highly polished mahogany counter that divided the comfortably furnished and pleasantly decorated room into two sections. There was carpet under their muddied boots that soaked in the water dripping from their long coats. Miss Kruger had been seated at one of the two teller positions behind the counter, a block of wood in front of her lettered with her name. Miss Vicary had been called away from the position marked with her name and was stooping over Albertson at his desk in the rear corner when the strangers entered the bank and pulled their revolvers.

The unshaven, weary-eyed, rain-sodden men all wore morose expressions for a moment, as Albertson and Faith Kruger rose from their chairs and Adele came erect. Then the safe with an open door, adjacent to the manager's desk, was seen by the men with the guns. Grins spread across their lean, sharp-featured faces at the same rate as terror gripped the rotund man and thin woman on the other side of the counter.

Faith Kruger took the first bullet in her flat chest and had time only to gasp softly before a second shot from the same gun entered her right eye, killing her where she stood. Adele Vicary started to scream in horror and bring up her arms, hands folded upright and fingers splayed in a pitifully futile effort to protect herself from the three bullets exploded toward her. The first shell blasted a hole in her belly, and as she looked down at the blossoming bloodstain on the fabric of her dress and reached with her hands to touch the wound two more bullets drilled into the crown of her head under her thin gray hair. It was not the first hit that made her into a moving target for the following shots; it was the forceful shove that Leroy Albertson gave her to get the elderly woman out of his way. But the little fat man with the suddenly wan face was not attempting to save her or himself from their hopeless situation. He too had a bullet in his flesh—from the gun of the third holdup man to fire. Leroy had taken it high in his right chest and its impact had caused him to abandon his groan of despair and growl a string of obscenities such as he had not voiced in years. He found he gained in determination from this profane outpouring . . . was able to ignore personal considerations of death as he heaved Adele aside and lunged from behind his desk toward the safe.

Miss Kruger was dead and down. Miss Vicary was dead and falling. All three men blazed their guns at Albertson now, and all three were venting gusts of laughter as they advanced on the counter to get clear shots over its polished top at the fat little man whose clawing hands dropped inertly less than twelve inches short of the safe.

The harsh laughter ended with a burst of hoarse coughing as the men sucked in the acrid taint of their own gunsmoke. Then the man in the center showed a scowl that was aped by the other two as he snapped, "Animal, check the street! Ives, let's collect!"

As the man who had triggered the opening shot of the massacre went to one of the windows flanking the door of the bank, Ives and the leader of the trio holstered their revolvers and vaulted over the counter. One began to snatch bills and coins from the tellers' drawers and transfer the money to the pocket of his long coat while the other went to squat before the safe.

"Sonofabitch!" Animal snarled, and pistol-whipped the unfeeling wall between the curtained window and the door.

"What now?" the top hand of the three demanded irritably without turning from his task of taking bills out of the safe.

"They stole our friggin' horses is what!" the man at

the window rasped back, yanking the curtain down from its fixing and pressing his face hard against the pane.

"Shit!" Ives groaned. "I'm done, Pierce!"

"No, maybe not!" Animal qualified. "Hitchin' rail's busted! Maybe the storm rattled them crazy critters and they broke loose and run."

"I'm through!" Pierce announced as he rose up off his haunches and turned away from the safe. "Douse that lamp!"

"Yeah, I see them!" Animal yelled in excitement as he craned his head around and pressed his face to the window. "Two of the bastards, anyways!"

There was a brass kerosene lamp at either end of the counter and Ives and Pierce acted in unison to extinguish both. A moment later, as these two men came back over the counter and drew their revolvers, a flash of lightning turned the false night into dazzling day again. The roll of thunder was a fraction of time later in coming and was marginally less deafening than that which had followed the last flash and masked the gunshots in the bank.

This clap and roll drowned out the distant crack of the lawman's gun as it was accidentally fired—a sound that would probably have been lost in the hiss of rain and the whine of wind anyway. In the transient brilliance of the lightning, Animal's shining eyes just failed to glimpse the hindquarters of the third horse as it bolted toward the intersection.

"Ain't none of them hicks left their critters anyplace nearby I can see, Pierce!" Animal rasped.

"We go for our own!" the top man ordered as he

emptied the spent shells from his Frontier Colt and slid fresh shells into the cylinder. The others imitated his actions, taking the reloads from the loops of their gun belts. Finally, Animal and Ives followed Pierce's example of drawing a second gun from a holster on the left side of their belts. "And we go now!"

"Wish I'd brought my friggin' Winchester in here!" Animal growled, the gleam fading from his eyes as he awkwardly turned the doorknob with a hand already holding a gun butt. He cracked open the door and inserted a foot between it and the frame.

"You called it, Animal," Ives reminded, obviously more tense than he tried to appear. "They're hicks out there. Be a whole lot more interested in keepin' their heads down than in shootin' our asses off."

Pierce had taken the time during the exchange to quell his own misgivings about this new and dangerous turn of events. So he was able to look and sound as coldly composed as an automaton when he told them: "It was a time ago I said now."

Animal, a grin reshaping his features again, kicked open the door so that it crashed violently against the wall. Pierce lunged outside, then Ives, and finally Animal. Each man rapped just one boot heel down on the hollow-sounding boardwalk before he landed with a splash in the mud of the street. Each raked his gaze and the muzzles of his gun barrels around a one-hundred-and-eighty-degree arc before he swung himself into a turn of half that much. Then, guns still drawn, all three hurried west along Main Street, despite the fact that they had seen one of their runaways galloping in the opposite direction. They chose this course because there was a large area of town filled with many unseen people and a slow-riding man out on the street between them and the horse. While at this end of town they had only to go between a dark-shrouded church and cemetery and three stores with lamplit windows before they reached the open trail where, maybe two hundred yards beyond the last building on the north side of Main Street, they had seen their other two mounts swing behind a stand of timber.

That building which the trio of running men had assumed to be the last one on this side of town was Quigley's Hardware, and Horace Quigley was renowned for inquisitiveness that often bordered on meddlesome snooping. His store had been emptied of customers by the storm and thus he had the opportunity to note the strangers' arrival in town, entry, and then exit from the bank. Rain on his own and the bank windows had badly obscured his view of the killings, but he had recognized the muzzle flashes for what they were. And so, when the lamps were extinguished, he was not surprised at what followed. And now, with the well-practiced sense of self-preservation of a man who had reached the age of sixty-eight through both hard times and easy, he waited eagerly until the trio were well advanced along the trail before he cracked open the door of his store, cupped his gnarled hands to his mouth, and roared: "Get Rich quick! Get Rich quick . . . the bank's been robbed."

The man called Edge, who had reined his mount to a halt alongside the jailhouse cell window in response to a harshly rasped call from Gideon Doyle, muttered sardonically to the Negro: "Figure that'll do it."

Chapter Three

THE PRISONER looked perplexed as he labored to work out what the stranger could mean by such a cryptic response to his opening: *"Hey mister!"*

But unlike Edge, Doyle had not seen the three gunmen lurch out of the bank, and had merely heard the shouting voice of Horace Quigley without comprehending what the hardware-store owner was yelling. Then, as a barrage of gunshots exploded toward the store at the far end of the street and he heard glass shattering, whatever the impassive-faced man astride the horse had said was of no consequence to the Negro. Doyle grinned and nodded his head vigorously, unfisted his hands from around the bars, slapped his thighs, and crowed amid the pandemonium that broke out in the wake of the gunshots: "I told that struttin' sonofabitch of a high-nosed lawman! I told him he was gonna have Animal trouble in this here town!"

The three holdup men made it to the blind side of the cottonwoods west of town where two of their horses had disappeared. This at the same time as doors were wrenched open along both sides of both streets. The more cautious of Loganville's citizens remained in cover to shout for information while the venturesome eased or plunged out into the rain to yell the same inquiries. Here and there somebody had thought to snatch up or draw a gun as he came outside.

The sheriff was the fastest man to respond to the emergency. He had been almost at the Blair house when he heard Quigley but failed to discern what the store owner shouted. He could not fail, though, to realize that somebody was shooting out window glass in his town. And he dumped the wailing and struggling Carrie to the mud-soft surface of River Road then turned to race back to the intersection, his Walker Colt drawn.

Doubtless because Edge was still astride his mount and thus towered above everyone else who had appeared in the streets, the lawman found his eyes drawn to the stranger as he came to a skidding and clumsy halt where the side street merged with the main thoroughfare. This after he had directed a perfunctory glance along the western stretch of Main and, impeded by the wind-whipped rain and burgeoning activity, been unable to spot any sign of what had happened.

"I'm Morrow!" he snarled. "Sheriff of this town! You see what that shooting and shouting was about, stranger?"

"Seems the bank's been robbed. Three men. Took off after their horses spooked by the storm. Threw some shots at somebody who yelled for you to come running,

Sheriff. Men and horses both went out of sight around the curve in the trail west.''

The man who made this even-toned and terse response to Rich Morrow's peremptory query was tall and lean and mean-looking, the sheriff decided. Two or maybe three inches over six feet and weighing something over two hundred pounds, with hardly an ounce of unnecessary fat. His face was as lean as his body and had more than a hint of the Hispanic in it. An ornery-looking face with narrow eyes—of a glinting blue, the lawman thought—and a long and thin, cruel set mouth. The nose was hawkish between high cheekbones and the skin that stretched tautly down to his aggressively cast jaw was dark stained by heritage and the elements— and cut deep with an intricate network of lines, visible even under a thick growth of bristles. Despite his unshaven state, it was possible to detect the outline of a Mexican-style mustache against the background of black and gray stubble. His hair, which was thick and worn long enough to reach untidily down to his shoulders, was more solidly black; but he was past forty and the graying process had definitely commenced.

He rode an undistinguished-looking chestnut gelding and sat a Western-style saddle hung with all the necessary accouterments for rough country travel, including a Winchester in a boot hung forward on the right side. His Stetson was black and so were his pants and his spurless riding boots. The rest of what he wore was obscured by a rain-sodden sheepskin coat with the collar turned up—except for the ties and toe of a holster that showed at his right thigh. A distinct bulge of the fabric above this indicated the tied-down holster was filled with a revolver.

His accent suggested that if he was not Kansas born and bred, he had spent a long time hereabouts, or maybe a littler further north.

From this first fleeting impression, Rich Morrow pigeonholed the stranger as the kind of man he least liked to have kicking heels in his town. But right now there was much more pressing business to attend to and he dismissed Edge from his mind. Just as he disregarded Gideon Doyle who jeered at him from the barred window.

"Wouldn't listen, Mr. Lawman! Like I told you, that Animal is a whole mess of big, bad trouble!"

The wind eased and the rain lashed less forcefully out of the sky that was still ominously dark. But the afternoon had less of a nighttime look now. The yelling back and forth was diminishing so that the clatter of feet on boardwalks and the more muted sound of other feet dragged through the sucking mud became dominant. There seemed to be a marked note of finality in a distant rumble of thunder after a flicker of lightning so far to the south hardly anyone in Loganville had noticed it. Certainly the stone-faced lawman remained oblivious to every aspect of the waning storm as he strode purposefully down the street, blue eyes fixedly staring at the rapidly expanding crowd of people out front of the bank.

The tall and stooped form of Horace Quigley came toward him, rattling fast words at everyone he passed but intent upon reaching Morrow. When the store keeper turned and fell in alongside the sheriff, Morrow listened with scant attention to the breathless words and nodded a great deal in a detached manner. He was distracted by stomach-cramping dread about how he would handle whatever awaited him inside the Loganville branch of the Kansas Mutual Trust Corporation. This was not the kind of town in which a peace officer had the opportunity to gain, much experience of such situations.

He shot a glance over his shoulder as somebody lit a lamp inside the bank building, his attention diverted by the plaintive voice of a woman, who pleaded, "Sheriff . . . Mr. Morrow . . . Lauren's still in the schoolhouse. The Nightingale boy says she was kept back with some others by Miss Heller. Did they go that way? The gunmen . . . did they go toward the schoolhouse, Mr. Morrow?"

The lawman had needed to make a conscious effort to maintain the hard set of his face and conceal his anxiety. Then, when he heard the dumpy and dowdy Emily Bass bemoaning the fact that her daughter was late coming home from school, he was in danger of giving in to genuine anger. But he saw in the concerned faces of the throng of people who had parted to allow Mrs. Bass through that he had best hear her out. And when she was done, Morrow discovered he was able to take a grip of himself and deal with the possibility that the schoolteacher and a bunch of her young charges might be in danger.

"They're all dead, Rich!" Ralph Eden announced in shocked tones as he stepped across the threshold of the bank and had to lean against the doorframe. "Miss Vicary and Faith Kruger and Albertson! Leroy looks to have been hit better than a dozen times! So much blood!"

"If it matters," Doc Corrigan intoned solemnly from

within the bank, silencing the babble of shocked talk triggered by the town butcher's revelations, "I make it ten wounds at the first count."

Morrow glanced at the front of the bank when Eden first spoke then returned his steady gaze to the grove of cottonwoods in which the Loganville schoolhouse was located. "Did you see those killers go by the school, Horace?"

The old man's eyes lost their brightness as he was called upon to provide information he was unable to give. "I tell you, Rich, after them outlaws was through shootin' out my store windows I kept myself low and down until I was good and sure they was through—you get my meanin'?"

Back along the street, Edge continued to sit astride his travel-weary gelding on the otherwise deserted intersection, waiting patiently for the black man to be done with his fervent babbling.

". . . soon as I seen that Animal and his two side-kicks ride in off the River Road, mister. Way it turned out, Mr. Lawman, he had other things on his mind by the time he come struttin' by here. Wasn't the chance for me to give him clear warnin'. But if there was, I bet that high falutin', tin-star-wearin' sonofanogoodbitch wouldn't have paid no mind to what—"

Gideon Doyle had been rattling out his opinions without regard to sounds that were washing along the street as the townspeople approached and merged with the smaller gathering that had first converged in front of the bank. But in the brittle silence triggered by the butcher's revelation about the killings, the black prisoner was provoked to interrupt himself. A morose expression quickly crowded enjoyment off his broad, bulging-eyed, fifty-year-old face. Then he growled softly: "Wish you hadn't done that, Animal. He was good to a damn fool nigger, was Mr. Leroy Albertson."

Edge shifted his narrow-eyed gaze back to the solemn face behind the bars after making a more detailed survey of Loganville's prime thoroughfare under a brightening sky as the wind ceased and the rain was reduced to a drizzle. "You wanted something, feller?"

"Uh?" Doyle grunted absently.

"You called me."

"I did?"

"After the horses and all hell broke loose and the sheriff went to take care of the kid in the mud."

The ebony face frowned in deep thought. And then Gideon Doyle snapped a thumb and finger. "Right, mister. Was gonna ask you—any service I can perform for you?"

"Not one," Edge replied baldly, and turned the gelding away from the cell window toward the Cottonwood Saloon.

"Name's Doyle, stranger!" the man in the cell called after him as he heeled the weary horse forward. "Gideon Doyle. Been almost three years since I blew into this town! Been general hand to a lot of folks around here ever since I reached Loganville! Ain't much I don't know about the town and the folks! More than that skinflint old snooper Horace Quigley is my claim! So anythin' you wanna know, you come to see me, mister! Pay me what you think's fittin'! And if you wanna give me somethin' on account, sir, I'll be willin' to accept it in kind! Since you're goin' into Mr. Snyder's fine

31

establishment! Mr. Snyder knows my brand of poison, sir! Just a way of speakin' . . . : a joke! Only the best is sold in the Cottonwood, sir!''

The black man's voice had gotten louder as Edge widened the gap between them. And the tone became huskier and more obsequious as he realized the stranger did, indeed, intend to go into the saloon—had turned his mount onto the boardwalk so that he could slide out of the saddle on to the planking rather than into the mud, before he hitched the reins to the rail out front of the red-brick-and-timber building.

The batwinged entrance was crosswise on the corner of the building, cutting off the point of the wedge. Edge paused before pushing through the slatted double doors to call across the street: ''I never take advice about liquor from men behind bars, feller!''

There was another burst of gunfire from the western end of Main Street, then a cacophony of raised voices and a furor of bustling movement. Edge merely glanced in that direction once again, his attention instinctively drawn toward the sound of shooting. But as he saw with indifference that this latest outbreak of violence had moved off the end of the street and on to the trail, his inclination to get done only what he had come to Loganville to do remained as firm as before.

A man leaning against the horseshoe-shaped bar said in a slurred voice: ''I'll tell you for nothin', mister. Just because I'm the only barber hereabouts don't mean I don't do the best I can. And when I'm sober, I'm damn good.'' He belched, thudded his chest, and continued: ''Pardon me, mister. Ain't sober now, but that don't make no never mind. On account of you figure yourself to be more in need of a drink than any barberin'. Am I right?''

Edge unfastened his coat buttons and took off his hat to shake water from its brim and crown as he advanced between the chair-encircled tables that were the sole features on one side of the saloon; on the other side there was a raised section at the rear on which stood a piano, a chair with a trumpet leaning against it, and another chair with a fiddle resting across its seat. Between the musicians' positions and the front of the stage there was enough space for a half-dozen dancing girls, provided their routine did not entail too much forward and backward motion. The stairway to the upper floor angled across the rear wall in back of the bar counter. There were two sets of beer pumps on the scarred, scorched, and stained bar top. Bottles and glasses were aligned on a counter-high section within the distorted half circle, set back far enough to allow two bartenders to pass each other without need to turn. There was not even one man behind the bar now. And the man who now said his name was Nathan Carlin and he was glad to meet the newcomer was the sole patron left in the Cottonwood after the disturbance on Main Street. Or maybe, Edge reflected with disinterest as he reached the bar, there had not been anybody else in there to be drawn outside. For it all looked neat and tidy in the light of four ceiling kerosene lamps—no disarranged chairs, half-finished drinks, butts on the floor, or abandoned playing cards on tables to point at an abrupt exodus.

In fact, the well-ordered appearance of the place served to underscore the disheveled appearance of the city-suited, bleary-eyed, slack-mouthed, florid-complected barber who was far too heavy for his five-foot three-inch height. He was perhaps forty-five and perhaps might drink himself to death before he was much older. He had to lean his hip and then his belly against the front of the counter and finally place both his hands flat on the top of it to keep from collapsing as he turned around to follow the course Edge took. With the instinct of the long-term drunk, he managed to avoid knocking over his empty shot glass.

"Am I right?" he repeated as he brought Edge into clear focus again.

"On the nose, feller," the tall lean man with the Stetson answered as he stepped behind a break in the bar near the foot of the stairs. He made a cursory examination of three bottles before he selected one and brought it with a shot glass to the closest table. Before he lowered himself with a sigh into a chair from which he was able to see both the batwing entrance and the stairs, he took a bill from a hip pocket and placed it on the table. He set the bottle on one end of the bill after he had filled the small glass.

Carlin watched all of this with intense concentration, glassy eyes fixed as he shook his head chidingly. Then he glanced dejectedly at what was left of his own drink and licked his lips after he watched Edge down the shot at a single swallow.

"Joe Snyder won't like you makin' free with his liquor, stranger," he warned as he made another fixed study of Edge pouring a second drink and setting the bottle down on the bill again.

"This is a sawbuck on the table here, feller. If

Snyder charges more than that for the amount of this rookus juice I plan to drink, he deserves to get gypped.''

Now, after a few moments of thought in the pleasant quiet of the saloon, Nathan Carlin nodded his agreement. ''Sure is right, and Joe Snyder don't overcharge, mister. Buy a shot off you for the fifty cents that's Joe's price?''

Edge was sipping the second drink, relishing its better-than-expected taste; the first shot had warmed the chill of the rainstorm out of his insides. He replied without rancor: ''I'm not in the saloon business.''

The barber looked like he was going to snarl a retort, but while he was endeavoring to think of one, he watched Edge and decided that it would be unwise to risk riling him. And he countered lamely: ''Suit yourself.''

''Usually do.''

Carlin endured the tranquillity for several seconds while Edge took out the makings and began to roll a cigarette. Then the barber snatched up his drink and tossed the final droplets of liquor against the back of his throat, thudded the glass down on the bar top. Complained: ''Shit, what's Joe Snyder foolin' at—runnin' out on payin' customers?''

''Maybe he forgot you're here and stopped by for a haircut,'' Edge suggested rhetorically, and struck a match on the tabletop to light the fresh-rolled cigarette.

''Anyone who knows me knows I don't do no barberin' after two in the afternoon!'' Carlin growled as if he had scored a point off the stranger. Then he experienced further hollow triumph as he glanced over his shoulder when he heard the batwings open and a heavy tread on the saloon floor, and was able to growl at the old-timer who entered. "You might as well scoot on down to the bank with the rest of them, Ira. Find out what all the ruckus is about. Snyder's run out on his business and we can't help ourselves on account of we ain't got the excuse of being strangers around here."

Ira Kyne, who ran the pig and chicken farm out along the River Road beyond the plank bridge, was at least seventy years old. He was short and slightly built and had a hollow-eyed, sunken-cheeked, prominantly jawed face. His hair was gray and so was his skin. He was dressed in a mud-spattered big apron with the cuffs of the pants pushed into high boots, a suit jacket that was perhaps three sizes too large for him, and carried a broad-brimmed straw hat that looked to have been chewed on by rats.

"Ruckus?" the old man asked with a perplexed expression and a loud voice that suggested he was hard of hearing, then nodded as he neared the bar. "Thought the town looked sort of empty even though the bad weather's near blowed out now. What's it all about, Nate?"

"Damned if I know, Ira. There was some shootin' and some shoutin' out the Dodge trail way. Snyder stepped out to see what it was all about. But he didn't come back inside to tell me before he took off with the rest."

Kyne only now seemed to become aware of Edge, and as he stopped beside Carlin at the bar he peered at the stranger like he was as shortsighted as he was deaf. Asked: "How about you, breed? You know anythin'—"

"He ain't no breed, Ira," the barber interrupted

anxiously. "Ain't Injun blood that makes him look the way—"

"Pa was Mexican and my ma was from north Europe," Edge cut in evenly. "Makes me a half-breed to my way of thinking, but I won't be called it by anyone else. And keep Mexican in mind. Any other name for my pa's nationality doesn't . . ."

He let the sentence hang unfinished as he saw a woman's head and shoulders show above the batwings. And tipped his hat but did not even half rise from his chair when she pushed between the doors. A tall, full-bodied woman with hair too yellow to be entirely natural and a round, once-pretty face that had been heavily powdered and painted to try to recapture a little of the good looks that had been lost during her near forty years of good living. But the recent harsh weather had ravaged her work before the mirror and deep lines of concern showed in her fleshy skin.

"Afternoon, Patsy, I was just sayin' to Ira here . . ." Carlin began as both he and the old-timer turned toward Carrie Blair's mother after seeing Edge react to her entrance. Drunk as he was, the barber could see the woman was the bearer of bad tidings. He altered the subject and his tone to ask: "You been to see what the ruckus is about?"

"Three saddle tramps just robbed the bank," she answered in a taut voice as she halted between the doorway and the bar, her long-fingered hands scrunching up the fabric of the oversize coat she had obviously hurried to don against the rain. "Killed Albertson and Faith and Adele. Now they're in the schoolhouse. Holding hostages and bargaining with Rich Morrow."

37

"Hostages?" Ira Kyne croaked, his head still screwed sideways-on to Patsy Blair as he strained to catch her every word and stared hard as if trying to see in the cosmetic-smeared features a hint of her thoughts. "Marvin didn't get home from—"

He interrupted himself when the woman nodded. Nathan Carlin, already considerably sobered by the deaths of his fellow citizens at the bank, gasped like a man parched by thirst.

"Yes, Ira," Mrs. Blair confirmed. "Your grandson. And Lauren Bass. Sam Dyer's girl—little Emily. And Kent Logan. Along with Arlene Heller, of course. The other children were let out from school early on account of the storm, but they were kept back for detention, according to my Carrie. Something to do with fooling around with ink and . . ."

Her voice trailed away as the old-timer came away from the bar, moving with a strange determined slowness, and then spoke in a harsh-toned whisper as he pulled the battered hat firmly on his head before he pushed between the batwings: "Morrow's dickerin' with a bunch of outlaw killers when there's childrens lives on the—"

The flapping doors masked the rest of what he said, and the silence that ensued made both Carlin and Patsy Blair uneasy. The man ended the pause with: "What's Rich doin', Patsy?"

"Him and a bunch of other men have got the school-house surrounded. All of them with guns."

A horse was heard to gallop up from the western end of Main Street then turn across the intersection and head along River Road with no slackening of speed and a great deal of vocal encouragement from the rider.

"Be young Ansel Twist riding out to Meadowlark to tell Spiro Logan," the woman supplied. "Guess Mort Bass will come on in with him. Mrs. Bass is already down there. Sam Dyer too. Told Rich Morrow I'd come get Ira. Knew it was about time for him to be heading for the Cottonwood."

She was talking for the sake of keeping the silence at bay. And Carlin endeavored to play his part in the same exercise.

"Hell of a thing to happen here in Loganville, Patsy. Leroy Albertson and those two old bid—and the Misses Vicary and Kruger gettin' killed. Hell, if it had been earlier on in the day, I might have . . ." He looked toward Edge as the half-breed's chair legs scraped on the floor. "I got my barberin' parlor right next to the bank."

"Appears to give the lie to what the temperance people would have us believe," Edge drawled, cigarette at the corner of his mouth, as he upended the empty glass over the top of the whiskey bottle that still stood on the ten-dollar bill. And concluded as Carlin eyed him quizzically: "It seems a man can stay clear of trouble by stepping into a saloon and taking a few drinks. Instead of the other way around. Sometimes, anyway."

"What's happened and what's still happening in Loganville isn't something to be taken lightly, stranger!" Mrs. Blair rebuked.

"Was speaking to the barber, lady," the half-breed told her evenly as he topped his hat again. "And talk doesn't get to be much more man to man than that."

39

She vented an unladylike snort of disgust as she dragged a chair from under a table and sat down wearily.

"I figure you'll be comin' back for more?" Carlin posed with a glance toward the table Edge had just left.

"For my change."

The barber suddenly looked eager. "Take your ten spot, mister. Have those two snorts on me. I'll settle up with Joe Snyder?"

"I pay my own way, feller. And I need the bottle left as it is so the bartender can see I took just the two drinks."

"So go to hell!" the wretchedly sobered-up drunk snarled after the tall, lean man who pushed out through the batwings.

"Too far down that trail to turn back now, I figure," Edge muttered.

Patsy Blair yelled in injured tones: "If Rich Morrow didn't have his hands full of more serious business, you'd get run out of this town for throwing your weight around the way you did and for insulting a lady!"

Her voice rang out shrill and clear in this part of Loganville where whatever sounds were made at the start of the Dodge City trail failed to reach. Then, after Edge had unhitched his gelding and remounted—again without stepping into the mud of the street—the prisoner did not even have to raise his voice for his words to carry to the rider.

"That Patsy Blair tells it like it is, mister! But it's my belief Rich Morrow would've bit off more than he could chew iffen he'd tried it."

There was no longer any rain in the unmoving air. The clouds were thinning and perhaps there would be some sun before it set. Edge kept a desultory watch on his surroundings as he turned his horse away from the saloon and headed across the street, paying no more attention to the tense and quiet gathering at the western end than to any other aspect of the small town that came within range of his glinting eyes. His well-developed sense for impending danger was not around; the majority of the town's citizenry was concerned with more serious matters than the presence of the man who merely looked like trouble waiting for the right time and place to happen.

Inside the Cottonwood, the full-bodied woman with the dyed yellow hair snarled: "*Mrs*. Blair to you, *boy*!"

The prisoner, who was at least ten years her senior, but black, showed his teeth in an indefatigable grin as the half-breed rode by the barred window, heading back east. "One thing a no-account nigger like me can be obliged to you for, stranger. Seems you rubbed them white folks in the saloon the wrong way." He laughed musically. "So I reckon you didn't put me down just on account of the color of my hide, right?"

Edge replied evenly with tobacco smoke trickling from the side of his mouth: "That's right, feller. I ain't prejudiced. I just don't like anybody."

Chapter Four

THE LOGANVILLE schoolhouse was a single-story building of gray stone set back from the trail in the center of what had once been a thick stand of cotton-woods. Much of the timber had been felled to form a clearing for the three-room building and the play yard in front of it. A four-foot-high wall of the same gray stone bordered the dirt yard on either side and at the trail frontage. A wagon-wide gap in this front wall was fitted with double iron gates that were solidly fixed in the open position by rust. Arlene Heller and a few of her more decorous students used the gateway to enter and leave the yard, but most of the youngsters leaped or scrambled over the wall at a more convenient point.

Some of the young people gathered into a tight-knit group at the point where the street became the trail beyond the cemetery and Horace Quigley's hardware store could recall their own rejection of the ill-placed gateway. The more elderly element could remember the felling of the trees, the work of the building, and the excitement of the day the new schoolhouse opened: all of it paid for by a bequest of Spiro Logan, Senior. Before that auspicious day, the children had been given their lessons in the less than ideal surroundings of the meeting hall with midtown hustle and bustle a frequent distraction to their studies. Loganville citizens of middle years were able to recollect working with primers and slates in the meeting hall on the south side of Main between the law office and Rankinn's Funeral Parlor and Chapel of Rest.

But if anybody in any age group was thinking along such lines as they waited for the next event in the chain started by the bank robbery, it was—either involuntarily or purposely—as a defense against far less agreeable notions.

None of them could see much of the schoolhouse from this point which Sheriff Morrow had designated as the closest that bystanders were allowed to come to the scene of potential fresh violence. The tall and skinny Quigley and the town butcher Ralph Eden had been charged by the lawman to ensure that the line was not crossed. And, in truth, there were few in the crowd who would have wanted to get any closer anyway. The tearful Emily Bass had needed to be forcibly restrained from dashing out along the trail. Old man Kyne, whose grandson was a hostage along with Lauren Bass, Kent Logan, the little Dyer girl, and the schoolteacher, had submitted to reason and did not need to be physically prevented from taking a hand in something best left to younger and more able men.

Rich Morrow, gaining in self-confidence to the point of arrogance, was the undisputed leader of the bunch of men he had quickly selected as soon as the seriousness of the situation at the schoolhouse was realized; he had gathered them around him by snapping out their names and then had taken the time to swear them in as deputies. Not all had thought to arm themselves when they came out onto the streets in response to the barrage of gunfire, but some men not deputized did have rifles or revolvers and they handed over their weapons without question.

Then, after Patsy Blair was sent to warn Ira Kyne what was happening and young Ansel Twist was instructed to saddle Kent Logan's pony and ride out to the Meadowlark spread with the news, Morrow assigned his inexperienced, angry, and apprehensive deputies to positions that established a cordon around the schoolhouse and yard.

At the front, crouched near the trail in the cover of the wall, was the powerfully built, leather-aproned, and bare-armed Sam Dyer. Abner Coburn, who like Dyer, was forty-five and was almost as tall but a lot thinner, squatted down against the wall close to the ever open gateway. The blacksmith and the liveryman were the only two members of the posse who could be clearly seen by the anxious audience on the end of the street. Sometimes caught sight of among the trees on the town side of the cottonwood grove were Joseph Snyder and Byron Pardo. Luke Farris and Ben Wade were hidden behond the wall in the timber. Lee and Oliver Rankinn, who were partners in their father's undertaking business, had been posted in the trees out back of the schoolhouse.

At first, Rich Morrow was constantly on the move,

checking that the men were in the positions he required
and had their weapons ready to fire. Feeling the need to
reassure them while he impressed on them the need not
to get trigger happy while the four innocent children
and the schoolteacher were held prisoners in the
schoolhouse. He made one part circuit around the sides
and rear of the building and yard, came back, and then
returned again. Came into sight at the far end of the
front wall from the watching crowd, across the unbarred
gateway from where the auburn-haired, freckle-faced,
beanpole-thin liveryman was squatting.

Just as his reluctant but determined deputies had not
queried what they were instructed to do, so the bystanders watched anxiously but with trust in Morrow's judg-
ment as the lawman came around the corner on hands
and knees and then squatted on his haunches like Coburn.
He no longer wore the Stetson and rain slicker and the
big Walter Colt remained in its holster since he had
commandeered a brand-new Winchester from the stock
of Harlan Monro, the Loganville gunsmith who had
premises between Ralph Eden's meat market and Ben
Wade's grocery store. Since Monro was away in Wichita visiting his married daughter, it had been necessary
to break into his place.

''Okay, you tough-talkin' hick-town lawman!'' a man
yelled from the cracked-open door of the schoolhouse.
''This is Pierce Starky and your time's up. Seen you get
us surrounded by a bunch of other hicks that look like
they don't know one end of a gun from the other! But
the only horse we seen was heading' outta town in the
wrong direction! And none of that is how we want
things, lawman! So you wanna ask the folks out there if

they got any preference as to which of the small fry gets it first?''

The voice was raised, but there was no tension in the tone as the leader of the trio of bank robbers issued the threat. And this only seemed to emphasize his determination far more than a note of strident fury would have done. Gasps, groans, then squeals, and finally a babble of alarmed talk accompanied his words. Until Animal roared, with unmistakable rage. ''And he ain't just flappin' his jaw to hear the sound of his own voice, you folks out there!''

This heralded a brittle silence, as if the entire world was waiting for some momentous event, responsibility for which would rest on the first person to utter a sound. High tension stretched time before Sheriff Richard J. Morrow trusted his voice to hold steady. ''Kill any of them you like. Any child or the teacher,'' he said.

Another rumble of alarmed talk from the body of watchers threatened to drown out what the lawman was saying. So he raised his voice, matching the composed tone of Starky, to drive his fellow citizens back into silence. ''But know this, you men! You shoot one of your hostages, you might just as well shoot all of them! We can only string you up once!''

''Rich—'' Coburn hissed through gritted teeth, his freckled face twisted by a grimace of revulsion.

''Shut up, Abner,'' the lawman answered softly but earnestly, head cocked in intense concentration.

''Don't be an asshole, lawman!'' Animal snarled, and burst into derisive laughter. ''We're already work for the hangman for blastin' the old folks at the bank

47

into the Promised Land! And they ain't the first we sent to the—''

A rasping interjection by one of the other men in the schoolhouse caused Animal to ease. Then Starky was clearly heard out in the trees and on the trail. "Figure you ain't forgotten what happened down at the bank, lawman.''

Morrow uttered a low grunt, which only he and Coburn heard, then answered: "As a lawman, it's my intention to arrest you for that and see you stand trial under due process of Kansas law. But anything happens to any of the kids or to Miss Heller, I intend to turn in my badge and lend a hand to anybody else with an itch to string you men up to the nearest tree. And we got no shortage of trees hereabouts.''

There was another tense silence that lasted for no longer than two seconds. Then a chorus of voices, male and female both, was raised in support of Morrow— before the noise was checked by Ives's taunting voice. "A hangin's a hangin' no matter where or how it's done, lawman . . . far as the guy that's gettin' hung is concerned.''

"If that's the way you see it, start killing your hostages!'' the grim-faced sheriff challenged.

Like Rich Morrow, the three men who had sought sanctuary and the means to bargain for their escape from Loganville in the town schoolhouse had removed their hats and their rain saturated coats. They were not so proficient as their adversary in concealing their true feelings, and so it was that the pretty young school-teacher and the four students she had kept in class were able to see Pierce Starky, Benedict Ives, and the man called Animal abruptly show a brand of fear that acted to intensify their terror.

"Pierce?" Ives groaned.

"You said—" Animal began.

"I know what I friggin' said!" the top man snarled as he raked his troubled gaze away from the frenzied faces of his partners to stare fixedly at the quaking Arlene Heller and the quartet of wide-eyed, lip-biting, wan-faced children.

When they had reached the far side of the cotton-wood grove and checked the barrage of shots that had kept the noisy old-timer quiet and cowering inside his store, the three men could see two of their mounts bolting out along the Dodge City trail through the teeming rain. Beyond the strand of timber and the low hillock across from it—which was the reason for the curve in the road west of Loganville—the country was Kansas flat. And the horses were showing no signs of slowing, putting yard after yard of dangerously open ground between themselves and the men in such dire need of reaching them.

Starkey pulled up first and the others skidded to a halt in the mud on either side of him.

"We'll never catch the lousy critters now!" Animal had snarled bitterly. He was thirty years old, five and a half feet tall, and weighed a flabby one hundred and seventy pounds. He had never been handsome but the scars of countless brawls made him positively ugly; there was stark white tissue above and below both his dark eyes, his nose and right ear were misshapen, his jawline was off center, and both his upper front incisors were missing. His remaining teeth were almost the same color as his matted brown hair. He had a weather-beaten complexion and was clean shaven when he took the time and trouble to shave.

"If we friggin' could, they'd be run ragged and no use!" Benedict Ives growled. He was a year or so younger than Animal, a head taller, and weighed about the same—but was built on leaner lines. He had a long, thin face with angular features upon which a smile did not rest easily. He was balding prematurely from the front, losing hair that was colored between blond and red. His eyes were green and very deep set and his teeth were very white and protruded. He affected a bushy mustache that was clearly visible even though he had not shaved for three days.

"So we get us some new mounts," Pierce Starky announced coldly, after briefly surveying the near empty length of Main Street again before he swung to the side and moved through the open gateway into the schoolyard. The top man of the trio was as tall as Ives and as broad as Animal, but his frame carried little excess fat. His age was thirty-five and his regular features and presently bristled but relatively unlined skin offered a true suggestion to the number of his years—this despite the fact that his short-clipped hair was mostly gray. He was clean shaven whenever he took a razor to the element burnished flesh of his face. It was the kind of face that, had there been some slight irregularities in the features, might have been handsome. As it was, when Pierce Starky looked his best, he presented a nondescript appearance that made him instantly forgettable—which had been a great advantage to him before he went into partnership with the squat and battered Animal and the cadaverously skinny Ives.

Breathing heavily after the exertion of the dash from the bank, Animal and Ives now hurried to follow Starky, all three of them searching the facade of the building with eyes cracked against the needling rain. They saw it was stone built under a low-pitched slate roof, single-storied, and stretched from one side of the walled enclosure to the other. There was a chimney up the outside wall at each end and another rose out of the ridge of the roof at the center of the building. The front entrance was also at the center—a wood door inside of a stone porch styled in a manner that caused Animal to demand: "What the frig we want with a church, Pierce?"

"Church is back there next to the bank," Ives growled. "Figure this place is a school."

"Shit, I thought it was horses we was after!"

"Maybe it's a ridin' school!" Ives countered, and vented a short, nervous laugh.

"Jokes he makes at a time like this!"

"Figure it shows I've got *class*."

Animal failed to comprehend the play on words and simply scowled, while Ives compressed his lips over his prominent teeth as if to tactily acknowledge that their situation was no laughing matter. Both of them were unaware of the grim smile of satisfaction that came and went from Starky's face as he neared the schoolhouse just as the storm started to abate. Starky could see that their luck was breaking even better than he had thought.

There were four sash windows in the front of the schoolhouse, two at either side of the porched entrance. Just two of these, immediately flanking the doorway, were angling wedges of lamplight out into the dark afternoon, and it was at the window to the left that Starky had seen from the trail the silhouette of somebody drawn there by the gunfire. Now, as he and his partners strode to within fifteen feet of the porch, their gazes and the guns in their fists unwavering while their unfastened long coats swirled and flapped in the diminishing wind, the watcher at the window was seen to be a woman. At the other lighted window there were two small girls and two boys.

"Shit, we can trade!" Animal rasped as his version of a grin rearranged the ill-used features of his face.

"Full marks, pal," Starky growled as he stepped into the porch and sent the door crashing open with a vicious kick.

The woman yelled something so shrilly it was almost a scream and lunged toward Starky with her arms flung wide, as if she was intent upon gathering up all four children.

Animal was hard on the heels of Pierce Starky, and Ives wasted no time in lunging over the threshold— fending off with an eblow the swinging door. Then he slammed the door closed and whirled to join the other two as they gazed and aimed their revolvers at the woman and children—the teacher standing with her arms angled out to the sides, shielding her charges from the intruders.

"Maybe you're Animal," the last man in murmured as his deep-set green eyes lit with appreciation of the woman's slender but distinctly curved figure, the lines of which were emphasized by the stance she had assumed.

"But I plan to make my own play to get to be the teacher's pet."

Arlene Heller was twenty-five and was definitely pretty rather than beautiful; her round and unremarkable face possessed that brand of youthful attractiveness that never outlasts girlhood. Her pale complexion was flawless, but her eyes were too round, her nose was snub, and her lips were a little too full. She did not make the most of her light brown hair that was bleached blond by the sun each summer—content to let it remain severely straight and keeping it cut short in a style that underscored the roundness of her face. Unlike her face, her figure, clothed in a plain skirt and only slightly frilled high-necked and long-sleeved blouse, had slimmed to fine proportions for her five feet ten inches.

The two boys, who were trying successfully to look like they disapproved of Miss Heller's protection, were about eleven or twelve, dressed in long pants and short-sleeved shirts. The girls, maybe nine and ten, were attired in a similar fashion as their teacher, except that their skirts were considerably shorter above high-button boots. The hands of all four children were heavily stained with red ink or dye.

"What do you want here?" the woman asked, her voice tremulous as her throat pulsed and the breath rushed out through her nostrils.

"Not you, schoolteacher," Starky growled, a little absently but with a degree of reassurance as he scanned their surroundings. "Not in the way Benedict Ives there made it sound. He just likes to make jokes. Nor any of the kids in that kinda way—Animal's called that because he's spent so long caged up behind bars in county jails and penitentiaries, and not for any other reason. I'm Pierce Starky and I'm a plain-speakin' man who does what he says he will. If the hicks of this town do like I tell them, you and the kids won't have nothin' happen to you that you won't have fun talkin' about when it's over.''

They were in a classroom furnished to handle twenty students, with ample room for double the number of desks and benches if the juvenile population of Loganville should demand it. The two windows at the front were matched by two in the opposite wall. At one end of the room was the teacher's desk and chair with a blackboard on an easel at either side of it. There was one closed door in back of the teacher's desk and another in the wall at the back of the room. Almost every square inch of what would have been bare, whitewashed wall space was masked by commercially printed or childishly executed maps and pictures.

''I want to go home, please sir,'' the redheaded girl with deep brown eyes said, her lower lip trembling as she struggled against the urge to weep.

''In a while, Lauren,'' Arlene Heller promised, and turned to face the children, stooping to the level of their strained faces. ''We'll all be going home very soon if we all do as we're told.''

''Get the lamps, Animal,'' Starky instructed as he moved around the teacher and students to go down the aisle between the desks and the wall, opened the door at the back of the room, and entered a half-size replica of the one they were in, with just a single window that looked out at the front. While Animal stood on desks to douse the two ceiling lamps that had been lit against the darkness of the storm, Starky moved along the aisle on the other side of the classroom—and grimaced as he saw the two windows looked out on a timbered area through which careful men might get dangerously close to the schoolhouse without being seen—particularly at night. At present, though, the level of light outside was getting brighter as the stormclouds broke. There was an unlit stove between the two windows on this side of the room, its stack climbing the wall and angling up the slope of the pitched roof. The door behind the desk and blackboards gave on to the smallest of the three rooms in which was stored furniture, books, and stationery.

"Pierce, there's a whole bunch of people out there!" Animal reported as Starky closed the door of the storeroom.

"Hicks, Animal, hicks," Starky answered, again taking out the two revolvers he had holstered while he made his check on the building. "No matter how many of them, we got the beatin' of them. Open the door a crack for me, pal."

Afraid, but managing to retain control over their emotions, all four children had quietly obeyed Miss Heller's calmly spoken instructions to return to their desks. Miss Heller was just sitting down on the chair behind her own desk, feeling relieved that the glittering-eyed and lip-licking Ives had not objected to what she was doing, when the ugly fat man at the window made his taut-voiced report.

Animal drew one of his handguns as he swung from the window to the door and fastened a fist over the knob, waited eagerly for Starky to close with him.

"Don't shoot them!" the teacher pleaded shrilly,

starting away from the chair, her tone and the expression on her face warning that her nerve was about to break.

The four children seated in a line of desks all sensed the depth of Arlene Heller's terror and called or cried out to her, knowing instinctively that if this woman they trusted lost control, the nightmare in which they were caught up would become much worse.

"Quiet them screamin' brats, Ives!" Animal raged, his excitement at the prospect of what Starky was about to do marred by the possibility that the children and their teacher might distract him.

"Okay, now!" the gray-haired man barked, his unmemorable face set in a sneer as he jerked his head at Animal.

Just for a second, Ives showed anxious indecision, his hands twitching as he aimed the revolvers at the near hysterical woman and the anguished children. Then Animal wrenched the door a few inches away from its frame. And Starky yelled: "Don't shoot them, Ives!" as he began to explode bullets out of the doorway, through the porch, across the yard, and over the wall.

The throng of townspeople with the sheriff at their head either turned to scramble away or ducked out of sight behind the wall. This as Benedict Ives, with a scowl of disappointment on his sharp-featured face, lunged at Arlene Heller, snaked his left arm around the back of her narrow waist to pull her tight against him, and raised his right hand to ram the muzzle of his revolver into the soft flesh where her jawbone came close to her earlobe. His move caused the woman and the children to catch their breath and silenced the shouting and screaming within the schoolhouse. Then, as Pierce Starky ended the fusillade and pushed forward a foot to prevent Animal from slamming the door, Ives made a half turn and his tightly held prisoner was forced to go with him. She whimpered in her helplessness and little Emily Dyer vented a truncated cry of alarm as the turn brought the gun in Ives's left hand to bear along the line of seated, ashen faced children.

"Shush, Emmy, or Miss Heller could be killed," Marvin James warned in grim tones and with a rebuking gaze.

"And that'd be a lousy waste of somethin' feels real good," Ives murmured, his discontent forgotten as he lasciviously held the trembling body of the woman hard against himself.

"You shot high, Pierce!" Animal complained.

"You people out there!" Starky shouted, leaning toward the open door and ignoring what was happening in back of him.

"This is Sheriff Morrow and I want to warn you—"

Starky pushed one of his revolvers through the gap, angled upward, and triggered a single bullet high into the brightening air. The report silenced the lawman and then Starky returned both guns to his holsters as he yelled: "You seen at the bank that we kill people! You got ten minutes to get me and my partners three good horses, saddled and with five days supplies in the saddlebags! You don't do that, we do some more killin'! One at a time until we get what we want! That's all!"

He withdrew his foot and signaled Animal to close the door. From outside, where dusk began to descend, Rich Morrow's angry voice reached across the yard.

57

But it soon became apparent that the men he demanded should surrender were paying him no attention and he was forced to abandon this approach.

Meanwhile, Pierce Starky grinned at the earnest-faced children and then ordered: "Let go of the schoolma'am, Ives, and get your mind up from between her legs. Let her sit in her chair again. You right- or left-handed, Miss Heller?"

"Right," she managed to whisper as she was released and sank onto her chair behind the desk. She kept swallowing hard and had to focus her gaze on the faces of the children for fear that she might forget her responsibility and collapse into self-pity.

"Then put your right hand flat on the desk, Miss Heller," the leader of the three brutal men said in a soft, almost gentle tone, and nodded in quiet satisfaction when she had complied without even a tacit query in her coal-black eyes. In the same low voice and with the grin back on his unprepossessing face, Starky added: "Okay, Ives. If the schoolma'am or any of the small fry make a peep, you bang up her hand real good, uh?"

Ives holstered one of his revolvers and altered his grip on the other so that he held it by the barrel. Arlene Heller clenched her right hand into a fist and then flattened it again, her eyes imploring the grimacing children to remain silent. Then Starky took off his sodden hat and coat and the other two followed his example, tossing the discarded clothes over vacant desks. Animal, at a signal from Starky, stood beside one of the windows at the rear of the schoolhouse. The top man took up a position near a front window and without haste extracted expended shell cases from both his guns and reloaded them. Then he kept an outwardly bored watch on the scene beyond the window, occasionally picking at his teeth with a filthy thumbnail and glancing at the clock that was fixed high on the wall at the back of the classroom. During the time it took for the minute hand to crawl around the short arc ordained by Pierce Starky, the monotonously measured tick of the clock sounded inordinately loud.

And thus did the tension-filled time pass until the gray-haired man stepped from the window to the door, cracked it open, and yelled out to Morrow—delivered the ultimatum that had drawn the shockingly unexpected response from Loganville's sheriff.

While Animal and Starky stared fixedly at each other, one man trusting implicitly in the second to take care of him, Benedict Ives took a hold of his revolver by the butt again and displayed his prominent teeth in a smile of keen anticipation as he looked down with glittering eyes into the terror-contorted face of Arlene Heller as the schoolteacher tilted her head to stare up at him.

"Pierce?"

"You said—"

"I know what I friggin' said!"

Ives's groan was heavy with something akin to sexual lust rather than tremulous with despair.

Animal was suffering a pathetic crisis of faith in a man who had never failed him before.

Pierce Starky at last managed to shake himself loose from the paralysis that had taken such an iron grip on him. He slammed the door violently closed and tore his gaze away from the pleading stare of the ugly Animal.

"Ives," he said, his tone milder than when he snarled the cursing retort to his other partner.

"Just give me the word, Pierce."

"The word is no."

"But—"

"I don't wanna get in an argument with you, Ives."

The continuing risk that Ives might explode a bullet into the pulsing neck of the terrified woman strengthened the other man's determination to remain self-possessed. At the same time, Starky's composure drew Benedict Ives back from the brink of wanton killing. The rigidity went out of his stance as he lowered his arm and slid the gun back in the holster; the carnal fire left his green eyes and his brutal grin became an amused smile.

"Not the time or place for quarreling, Pierce," he allowed.

"Glad you see it that way, pal."

The two young girls and slightly older boys remained tense and silent, totally unresponsive to the tall, thin, no longer patently dangerous man who smiled at them and said, "Not in front of the children."

Chapter Five

EDGE ATTENDED to the feeding, watering, and bedding down of his own horse in the well-equipped and well-run livery stable with a small shingle on one of the double doors that proclaimed ABNER COBURN ESQUIRE, PROPRIETOR.

When he entered the place, which was on the south side of Main, he found it unattended and assumed the liveryman was engaged with the trouble on the far side of town. Rather than kick his heels waiting for a man to come by and take care of chores he was quite capable of handling himself, the half-breed made the travel-weary gelding as comfortable as the four other horses already in the stable. As he inserted another ten-dollar bill in a rigging ring on his saddle that was hung from a peg at the front of the gelding's stall, he muttered: "Going to see a man about a horse, and you're it, feller."

Then he doused the kerosene lamp that Coburn had

left lit and closed the livery door behind him. As he walked along the street, he heard some more shouts and a chorus of voices raised in dismay down where the Dodge City trail began. He was aware of being under surveillance from the line of houses across from the stable, the place where Byron Pardo treated sick animals and pulled human teeth and from the town carpenter's workshop. But he was unable to discern any hostility in the silent study and thought that the watchers were most likely children confined inside by elders who had scurried off to experience the vicarious excitement that can be gotten from other people's tragedies.

There were no sidewalks on this stretch of Main Street and trudging through the mud was disagreeable to somebody who considered horseback riding the only fitting mode of travel. But the half-breed, who had his hands in the pockets of his sheepskin coat, was accustomed to enduring far worse than a short walk down a muddy street on a chill spring evening. And the impassive set of his lean, dark-skinned, glinting-eyed face revealed nothing of what he thought about his present circumstances. This was, more often than not, the way he responded outwardly to most situations—good, bad, or any shade of neutral.

Beyond the vacant lot next to Luke Farris's workshop, Gideon Doyle was peering out of his cell window, cheek pressed hard to the bars to catch a glimpse of the approaching stranger. The moment he recognized Edge, the black man began to say earnestly: "Thought that'd be you, mister. Put your horse in Coburn's livery is my guess? Fine place for a horse to be. Mr. Abner Coburn, he runs a real nice stable. I help him out now and then.

Sweepin' up or totin' bales up into the hayloft and such like. Like I helps most folks around town. Do chores real good, you can ask anyone in Loganville. I want you to know, mister, that I didn't do nothin' real bad to have Mr. Morrow arrest me. All I done was drink a couple more than I should've and tried to play the piano in the Cottonwood . . . so they say and I ain't disputin' that's what I did. I can't play the piano, mister. But seems I thought I could and I just kept thumpin' away at it and wouldn't stop until Mr. Morrow was brought and . . ."

Edge had merely glanced at the eager face behind the bars as he drew level with the window and treated the fast-talking man to an almost imperceptible nod of acknowledgment before he went on by. Doyle began to talk even faster and a great deal louder in his zeal to have the half-breed know he was of proven good character, despite his present circumstances.

"Know where to find you if I need you," Edge called back over his shoulder as the Negro's explanation ground to a halt.

Then Doyle bellowed: "Watch out, mister!"

The half-breed had been distracted by Doyle's impassioned plea for sympathy. But at the same moment as Doyle roared the first word of the warning, Edge felt the itch between his shoulder blades and a hot spot at the nape of his neck. He was past the law office by then and at the front corner of the meeting hall—opposite the start of River Road with the South Wind Hotel on one corner and the Cottonwood on the other. When Edge came to an abrupt halt, half turned from the waist to look over his left shoulder, he knew with the certainty of long experience that the threat was posed from that River Road area. His half-shut eyes tracking along the area, he decided the alley between the law office and the frame meeting hall offered safer cover than the buildings, which were closed and might be locked.

In the part of a second it took Gideon Doyle to yell the warning, Edge was poised to make his move: to swing his right leg around and push off with his left into the alley mouth, hands wrenching from his pockets so that one could tear open the coat fastenings while the other clawed the Frontier Colt from the holster—if one or more bullets did not drill into his back or his head at the instant he started the turn.

"Move a muscle and you're dead, stranger!" Nathan Carlin ordered.

Edge was conscious of holding himself in a state of suspended animation for stretched seconds. And for part of this short time, as he heard footfalls on the sidewalk across the street and the flapping of the saloon's batwing doors, the strain was painful—ached so intensely his features showed a grimace. With a scowl, he acknowledged that the town barber would try to kill him only out of fear. Then, as the tension drained from him, his features re-formed into their usual impassive expression.

"You're crazy drunk the both of you," Doyle accused in strangled tones as the half-breed ignored Carlin's decree, and kept his hands pushed deep into the pockets of the sheepskin coat as he peered phlegmatically across the muddy street in the gathering gloom of evening.

The short, fat, florid-faced man in the city suit was wearing a derby hat now. He stood outside the saloon entrance, right shoulder braced against one of the posts supporting the second-floor balcony. An old Spencer carbine was nestled against his other shoulder and his cheek was pressed to the stock as Carlin drew a bead on Edge. Patsy Blair was to the side and behind the barber, her back against the batwings as if she was ready to hurl herself through at the first sign of danger. She had shed the oversize coat and could now be seen to be dressed in a plain and simple gown that fit tight enough to her fleshy body to contour the substantial undergarments she wore.

There was excitement on her once pretty face and she seemed to be rasping low-toned encouragement to Carlin, whose own puffy features were largely obscured by the carbine.

"You shut your impudent mouth, boy!" the woman snarled.

"Wan . . . want to know . . ." Carlin had to swallow the nervousness that had risen in his throat. ". . . know what you got in mind to do, stranger?"

Edge gave a curt nod and replied: "No sweat, feller. Going to tell you to stop aiming that carbine at me. And warn you that if you ever have occasion to point any kind of gun at me again, shoot to kill."

"Tough talk doesn't cut no ice with me, mister!" the woman with the too yellow hair snarled. "Nathan Carlin means what are you planning to do down where all the trouble—"

"Right!" the city-suited, derby-hatted Carlin cut in.

"Because I'll kill you if you don't," Edge continued as if there had been no interruptions. "Having guns aimed at me riles me. Try to give folks the one warning if I'm able. And I'd be obliged if you'd let it be known to the other folks around here. On account of there being so much shooting off of guns in this town."

"I'll do that, mister!" Gideon Doyle promised enthusiastically. "I'm due outta here in a couple of hours and I'll see the folks gets to hear—"

"Shut up, Doyle!" Carlin roared.

"I told you, nigger!" Patsy Blair snarled.

It had been two or three minutes since sounds of any consequence had come from the people down at the western end of Main Street. But the standoff between the three men in the schoolhouse and the intractable sheriff continued to hold their undivided attention. Only the Negro prisoner and the children in the houses on Main Street and River Road witnessed the second potentially explosive situation in Loganville.

Then galloping hooves could be heard far off in the gathering darkness as Nathan Carlin overcame his apprehension and moderated his tone after his snarling rebuke of the black man. "I believe what you've told me, stranger. But with the lives of a bunch of little kids on the line and a man who looked like another mess of trouble headin' on down toward—"

"The grocery store, feller," Edge cut in.

"Uh?"

"Where I was headed for when you made this stupid play. And had it in mind to place an order there for supplies to pick up before I leave this town tomorrow. All of which is my business."

The sound of hooves thudding into rain-sodden ground swelled in volume as the group of fast riders approached

Loganville on the trail that crossed the plank bridge over Sunflower Creek.

Patsy Blair, stepping away from the batwing doors and peering toward the horsemen, said something to Carlin that caused him to swing his head away from the carbine stock and glance in the same direction.

The half-breed did not lunge for the protection of the night-shadowed alley now. He only yanked his hands out of his pockets and jerked the side of his coat up.

Nathan Carlin, distracted by the galloping horses and what Patsy Blair told him about them, almost squeezed the carbine's trigger when movement on the periphery of his vision snapped his full attention back to the tall, lean man on the other side of the intersection. Had he done so, he might well have killed the man called Edge. Who was still swinging around from the waist and bringing up his right hand, thrusting it out, fisted to the butt of the Colt, which was cocked before the muzzle cleared the holster.

Then it was too late. For Edge was as immobile as a rock, petrified in a pose of menace that so stirred the fear of death in Carlin that he began to tremble. And might well have found it difficult to stay on his feet had he not been leaning on the post. The carbine wavered like the slender limb of a tree in a capricious breeze.

"Get rid of it!" the half-breed yelled, raising his voice so he could be heard against the beat of hooves as the riders galloped into sight.

Carlin wrenched the Spencer down from his shoulder and flung it forcefully into the mud. The glow emanating from lamplit windows showed the dread that was etched into the face of the little fat man as he thrust his hands high in the air. Patsy Blair uttered a sigh of anger when she saw his surrender.

The shrill laughter of Gideon Doyle was heard for a second or so before it was drowned out by the hoof beats of five horses racing off River Road onto Main Street. None of the riders reined in his sweat-lathered mount and there was a danger of them plunging into the press of people near the schoolhouse. Possibly all the riders were too concerned with other things to pay close attention to the man at the side of the intersection as he pushed his Colt back in the holster. And certainly none of them had cause to glance over their shoulders at the saloon entrance where Nathan Carlin remained with his arms up high until the furious blonde snarled at him to bring them down. Then the Negro's gleeful laughter was brought to an end by a fit of coughing as the beat of hooves faltered and the hell-for-leather ride finished with a flurry of rearing and shying, snorting and whinnying.

"Go right on choke yourself, nigger!" Patsy Blair sneered at the only target for her rage who was in no position to retaliate as voices were again raised in anger and consternation at the far end of the street.

"God, do I need a drink," Carlin groaned, staggered into the saloon.

"What about Snyder's gun?" the woman yelled at him as the batwings flapped in his wake. "He'll be mad as hell if we don't clean it up and put it back under the bar, Nate!"

The barber said something brief and perhaps obscene. It failed to carry clearly across the intersection, but Patsy Blair heard it plainly, and from her expression as her lips moved, she probably responded in like manner, but under her breath. Then, obviously aware she was being closely watched by the half-breed, who had not moved from the spot where Gideon Doyle's shout had halted him, she stooped and lifted the carbine out of the mud. In coming upright, she was careful not to soil her dress. Then she turned, carried the gun gingerly into the Cottonwood, and, from out of sight beyond the batwings, yelled: "If you hadn't acted so hard-nosed since the trouble started, we wouldn't have—"

"Leave it, Patsy!" Carlin admonished her, harsh but weary.

"It's my opinion, mister, that actin' don't have a thing to do with the way you are," the Negro called through the bars, still happy. 'You're hard 'cause that's the way you are and ain't no help for it. And somethin' else: I ain't seen no one that was faster with a gun—that didn't take the time not to pull the trigger. You get my meanin'? And I been around some for a no-account nigger boy."

"Yeah, feller," the half-breed replied as he continued to trudge along the street. "And I ain't saying that you're wrong—but not all of us are as black as we're painted."

Chapter Six

GIDEON DOYLE'S joyful laughter rang out shrill in the lamplit evening, counterpointed by the slapping sounds of his hands against his thighs. Until Patsy Blair yelled a harsh command that he should stop.

Beyond the meeting hall on the side of the street where Edge was walking was the Rankinn Funeral Parlor and Chapel of Rest, Nathan Carlin's barber shop, the recently robbed Loganville branch of the Kansas Mutual Trust Corporation, and the cemetery and church. There were tree-shaded vacant lots between the single-story buildings and the bank was exceptional in having a stoop. Edge elected to angle across to the north side of the street where there was a line of stores and businesses with an uninterrupted run of roofed sidewalk at the front. Wade's Grocery was at the center of the block, next to the broken-open gunsmith's and immediately opposite the bank.

Just as the half-breed reached the threshold of the grocery, a man called: "Neither Ben nor his wife are in the place, mister! Down to the school with the rest. Including my boys, who got deputized and are standing guard. When they should be here lending me a hand with the deceased!"

Rankinn, the town mortician, had stepped into the doorway of the bank. Edge saw him to be a tall, slender man of close to sixty with hardly any gray hair and a lush but neatly trimmed beard. He was appropriately dressed for funereal chores: in black with a white shirt. The expression on his rugged face matched his tone of voice—embittered rather than mournful.

Edge answered: "There's a feller in the jail who's due out soon and needs to earn a couple of—"

"He'll get to help with the digging of the graves," the mortician growled as a short and broadly built, muscular-looking woman in her late middle years hurried along the boarding, her heels rapping noisily. She had a hard-set face that was emphasized by the suspicion she directed at the half-breed. "That there's Clara Wade coming—"

"Clara Wade I am and I'm coming to close up the store!" the woman interrupted, intending both Rankinn and Edge to receive an equal share of her indignation. Her resolute approach had caused the half-breed to pause once again at the doorway of the store, and as he looked toward her he saw that she was the first of many people who were leaving the crowd at the start of the trail, men and women both, but none in as much haste as the almost square-shaped Clara Wade. Two men were leading the five sweat-lathered horses that had been ridden into town a few minutes earlier.

"Ben's been deputized as well as your boys, Elmo Rankinn!" the woman went on resentfully. "And Abner Coburn, Joe Snyder, Luke Farris and Byron Pardo. Rich Morrow's got it well in hand and now that Mr. Logan is here with some of his men, it's my feeling it'll all be over before long. With no more work for you."

She had reached the doorway of the store and Edge stepped aside for her to go inside, tipping his hat. She did not acknowledge his gesture as she swept by him with a swish of her severely styled dark gown and waist apron, but did make the effort to direct a rancorous glare across the street at the mortician.

"Those killers'll be taken to Wichita for the trial and be hung there, mister. So the Rankinn family won't make no money out of their carcasses." She moved across the cluttered store that was filled with countless smells, all of them appetizing, and began to straighten up the disarray her husband had left when he joined the hue and cry after the killings. She moved her hands as fast as her walk had been and her talk still was. "There's some that say undertaking is a job that has to be done in this day and age, but that never will be my feeling. In the old days, a family took care of burying its own. Or pitched in to help if the neighbors had need. Fine if a preacher was close by to say the words. If not, there was always someone could read something out of the Good Book. Don't hold with anybody making money out of other folks' grief and tragedy."

"What's your feeling about making a few dollars out of a man's hunger, lady?" Edge asked as the scowling woman began to stow packages, cartons, and sacks beneath the counter and on shelves.

"What?" she asked absently, as if she only now became aware that there was a customer in the store. "Oh. Yes, you want something. My husband's busy with law business right now and—"

A stream of people were now passing the store and the clatter of their booted feet on the sidewalk and the snatches of talk that were heard through the open doorway provided a frequent distraction for Clara Wade, even after Edge had reminded the woman of his reason for being in the grocery.

"Like to give you a list of what I need, lady. Plan on staying in town tonight and leaving for Dodge in the morning. What time could my order be ready?"

"What is it you want?"

The half-breed knew the woman was running out of steam. Her eyes were becoming duller by the moment, she swallowed a lot, and her tone had lost its acerbity. Her fellow citizens going by the store had been reduced to a trickle now. And it was obvious that she had been hoping to see her husband turn into the doorway—or, if not him, somebody to tell her the trouble at the schoolhouse was ended peacefully.

"Here," Edge answered, and took a dirty and crinkled strip of paper from a pocket of his shirt. He unfolded it and placed it on the counter. "Used it a few times, but it can still be read, ma'am. Nothing out of the ordinary. Coffee, flour, beans, beef jerky. It says how much of each. If you don't stock anything on the list, I figure you'll know a place in town where I can get it. Or I can hold out until I reach Dodge."

Mrs. Wade scanned the grubby-looking shopping list apathetically, then nodded. "If Ben's kept busy with the law work, I can fill this for you. If nothing bad happens, the store'll be open at nine. You can pick up the order at a quarter after. I'm not sure about the prices, so I can't tell you what it'll all cost."

"I'll know if I'm being overcharged," he told her, and tipped his hat as he turned from the counter.

He knew that a few minutes earlier she would have bristled at his words and hurled a steam of abuse at him as he left the store. But she did not, in fact, offer any parting comment. He could not be certain, for he did not look back, but he thought he heard Clara Wade vent a stifled sob.

There was just a small group of people beyond the western end of Main Street now, clearly seen in the light of a half-moon that sometimes glowed less brightly as thin and ragged clouds drifted across it. Most of the townspeople were now back from the trail. Just a few, in pairs or threes, lingered in the open, perhaps fearful to be alone. The somberly clad, bitterly frowning Elmo Rankinn still stood sentry over the bullet-shattered dead in the bank. He felt the need to call across the street, his tone even: "You doubtless don't care one way or the other, young man, but you shouldn't judge the folks of Loganville by the way they are this evening."

"You're right, feller."

"I'm glad."

"I don't care one way or the other."

"The hell with you!" Rankinn said, without vehemence.

The dumpy and dowdy Emily Bass and another middle-aged woman with a finer figure and a far less distraught look were the only females left on the moonlit trail. The two of them stood close together and slightly apart from the men, the more composed woman poised to comfort the agitated Mrs. Bass if it proved necessary. While Mrs. Bass, the mother of one of the student hostages, never shifted her gaze from the cottonwood stand out along the trail, her companion and the six men nearby all glanced toward Edge when they heard him approach. Whether or not they recalled that he was the recently arrived stranger, none of them felt him worth more than a perfunctory look before reverting to the shadowed timber in which stood the schoolhouse, no lights showing at any of its windows.

Edge attached himself to the group of men and began to roll a cigarette after he had peered toward the focus of apprehensive interest. He saw one man crouched on the trail close to the gateway in the wall and three more posted in the trees on this side of the school.

"Mister?" the tall and skinny Horace Quigley posed, shuffling up close to the half-breed without shifting his gaze away from the cottonwood grove. "Am I wrong, or did I see that Nate Carlin get the drop on you."

"You're not wrong."

"Didn't I say that's what happened?" the owner of the hardware store snapped in the manner of somebody scoring a point, and swept his gaze over his companions in search of a deserved acknowledgment. "My eyesight ain't all that bad and—"

"Shut up, Horace!" a dungaree-clad man who had the look of someone sick to his stomach groaned miserably.

76

"Yeah, button your mouth or get the hell away from here, Quigley," a man who was dressed—and smelled—like a blacksmith added. Then immediately seemed to regret what he had said as he muttered: "Carlin was too liquored up to know what he was doin' anyway, is my guess."

"Drunk for sure," the wizened Ira Kyne agreed. "And egged on by that Blair woman, I bet."

"That woman—" the one comforting Emily Bass began in a tone of reproach.

"Mrs. Sullivan," the man Edge presumed to be Logan cut in sharply, then curbed his initial irritation. "Mr. Quigley, Mr. Dyer, Kyne. And you, Mort . . . isn't there enough trouble in this town right now that you can't set aside personalities and forget your prejudices for—"

Logan was in his mid-fifties, a broadly built man of a little less than six feet in height, muscular once, perhaps, but starting to run to fat now. He had distinguished good looks with a tanned complexion that was emphasized by the whiteness of his hair. His teeth were very white too and his eyes were light-colored and showed clear and bright in the glow of the moon. He wore a cream-colored Stetson and the rest of his clothing was Western fashion—shirt, kerchief, vest, pants, and heeled boots with spurs. He also wore a gun belt with an ivory-butted, plated Remington in the holster. Like the revolver, all his clothing was of high quality; worn for style rather than heavy-duty wear. Although his hands had done a lot of hard work in the past, they had softened and swelled of late, and the stone-studded rings on the third fingers of each hand had sunk into the flesh.

"Sheriff's comin' back, sir," the sixth man in the group interrupted deferentially. He was about thirty and was attired in the workingman's variant of Spiro Logan's outfit. His clothing, the frame it was fitted to, and the face above looked to have seen more hard times than easy.

They all seemed briefly relieved that Morrow's emergence from the cottonwoods would bring their exchange to an end. A few looked discomfited, perhaps because a man they held in high regard had just taken them to task.

The striking of the match by Edge on his gun butt was startlingly loud in the tense silence and brought to a sudden end the group's momentary peace of mind. Many eyes directed fleeting resentment at the flare-lit face of the half-breed as he touched the match to his cigarette, then turned to the tall and lean figure of the lawman, who came out of the trees warily but then moved along the trail in a stiffly upright gait that was almost a strut.

Morrow's expression of near arrogant self-confidence was for a moment displaced by a frown as he recognized the stranger; he had taken an instant dislike to Edge when he first saw him at the start of the trouble. But he quickly recovered his composure as he asked: "You want something here, mister?"

"Need to see three of the fellers in your posse, Sheriff. Let them know I'm doing business with them and—"

"The hell with all that, Morrow!" the dungaree-clad

man snarled. "While my little Lauren's still in the hands of them three killers I ain't gonna stand around here listenin' to you throw your weight—"

"Hush up, Mort," his wife urged.

"No, he's right, Mrs. Bass," Sam Dyer, the blacksmith, countered, then said to the half-breed: "No offense, stranger, but whatever business you got in this town'll have to wait. We got big trouble with the schoolteacher and four kids—"

"The man knows," the ragged-garbed Ira Kyne cut in. "Was at the Cottonwood when the Blair woman come to find me and tell me what was happenin' out at the school."

"I bet that liquored-up Nate Carlin figured you was part of the bunch that's—" Horace Quigley put in eagerly.

"Let's not get started on that tack again!" Spiro Logan interrupted, his expression grim and his tone of voice authoritative as he raked his light, bright gaze over everybody in the group. Finally locked eyes with Morrow and demanded: "You've told the men and they understand, Sheriff?"

Just for part of a second the lawman allowed his wounded pride to show; Logan had made it blatantly obvious that he outranked the lawman in the present circumstances. Then he became wooden-faced as he responded: "Yessir, Mr. Logan. Every member of the posse knows you're supporting my stand—"

"And that Ira and me ain't?" Sam Dyer growled.

"And Mort's only backin' you on account of he works for Mr. Logan at the Meadowlark spread and so—' the old-timer who ran the pig and chicken farm added in a similarly disgruntled tone.

"I wasn't told to tell them that," Morrow interrupted, his tone as dispassionate as his expression as he took the opportunity to acknowledge that he was no longer top man—and to renounce responsibility for what might go wrong. "Did tell them that almost the entire town of Loganville is against giving the killers what they want—and that was no lie." He looked pointedly at Dyer, Kyne and Mort, and Emily Bass, then grunted when none of them took issue with him. Returned his gaze to Spiro Logan and continued in the manner of a junior officer making a report to his superior: "All the men know how vital it is to keep a sharp lookout, sir. And that they are only to open fire if they are one hundred percent certain it will save the life of one of the hostages."

"They've seen nothing of what's taking place inside since darkness fell?"

"No. The lamps are still out. And nobody's even smoking in there."

"Nor heard anything?"

"A little moving about. Some talk, but not loud enough for what was said to carry outside. Seems they know it's a stalemate, Mr. Logan."

The rancher had nodded a great deal while he listened to the lawman. Now, his grim-set face hardening toward a scowl, he shook his head slowly as he murmured: "By the very nature of such a situation, Sheriff Morrow, it works both ways."

The lawman, seeing Logan's lapse into despondency

as a sign of weakness, was almost triumphant as he countered: "Until one side is worn down and surrenders."

Several members of the group were about to add to the exchange, but somebody removed from them spoke first: "Hey, you men in the school?"

It was loud, commanding, and yet with a note of fear. In the surrounding silence it was easy for the surprised people on the trail to pinpoint the position of the man who now added, unnecessarily: "I'm over here on the rise!"

"Shit, it's Rod," the ranch hand beside Spiro Logan rasped.

"That's Rod Potts," Horace Quigley hissed at Edge, who had been about to swing around and head back into town. "This is his brother Glen. Rod Potts and Arlene Heller been walkin' out for a while. Arlene Heller is the school—"

"For God's sake, hush your mouth, why don't you, Mr. Quigley?" Emily Bass urged with weary fervor, probably forestalling several other rebukes that would not have been put so courteously.

Edge nodded at what the elderly town gossip had told him and then did a double-take toward the figure he had glimpsed as he began his move away.

"Young Ansel Twist who works at the stage-line depot," Quigley hurried to inform the half-breed—careful to keep his voice low—as he too spotted the skinny youth standing tentatively in front of the bullet-shattered facade of his hardware store.

"You gonna answer me?" Rod Potts yelled, louder than before, the quiver of nervousness even more evident. As he pleaded for a response he reached the base of the grassy knoll opposite the schoolhouse and came to a halt. "I ain't got no gun but I'll keep my arms high until you say I don't have to!"

"Crazy young fool," Logan muttered.

Quigley leaned his face so close to the half-breed's head that Edge could feel the old-timer's warm breath against his ear. "Potts and Ansel was sent to take the horses well clear. In case the killers made a break and got them."

The man making the lone play now took a half-dozen paces forward, moving out of the moon shadow of the rise and making himself a vulnerable target. From a distance, he looked to the glinting eyes of Edge to be an identical twin to Glen—certainly both had rangy frames and were dressed in the same workaday ranch-hand manner—except Rod was minus a gun belt.

"Rod, what are you doing?" Arlene Heller shrieked, her voice ringing out so distinctively that it was apparent the door or a window of the schoolhouse had been opened.

"No one told you to flap your trap!" Benedict Ives snarled.

And there was the sharp crack of a vicious blow on bare flesh. Then a shrill cry of pain. Rod Potts made to lunge for the gap in the wall but froze in a forward-leaning attitude as a gunshot once again split the Loganville night. During the second he was thus transfixed in a posture that came close to defying gravity, many thought the bullet had hit him. His brother made to dash out along the trail and Abner Coburn sprang from his crouch at the base of the wall beside the gateway.

"I hear you and see you, punk!" Pierce Starky snarled. "And if I gotta fire again, I won't aim over your stupid head!"

Potts rocked back onto his heels and became rigid. Coburn sank down on to his haunches again and Glen shook free of the restraining grip that Rich Morrow had fastened on his upper arm, then shuffled backward with a bitter snarl instead of resuming his charge along the trail.

"I wanna make a deal!" the man in the open with his arms thrust high in the air again announced.

"I don't see no horses saddled and ready to ride, punk!"

"That's between you and Rich Morrow! I want you to let Miss Heller go and take me in her place!"

There was some laughter from within the schoolhouse that perhaps acted to drown out the venting of other emotions by the teacher and her students.

Emily Bass muttered bitterly: "Fine thought, son, but what about the children?"

"Reckon I can help there, woman," her husband growled, and the resolution in his face and the way he clenched his hands warned Morrow not to impede him as he stepped forward.

"I'm with you, Mort," the blacksmith said earnestly, and added actions to his words.

"Count me in, boys," Ira Kyne said thickly, and jammed the battered straw hat back on his head as he fell in alongside the other two.

Mrs. Bass vented a choked cry of despair mixed with pride as she accepted the supportive embrace of Mrs. Sullivan. This as Morrow, looking sick to his stomach and desperate, stared at Spiro Logan and rasped: "What'll we do?"

"We want friggin' horses, not friggin' heroes!" Starky yelled. "And ain't no one gonna leave here or come in until we got what we want! So get the hell away from here and tell that sheriff he better—"

"Pierce, there's more comin'!" Animal shrieked as two fathers and one grandfather of three of the child hostages advanced far enough along the trail to be seen through the timber. By accident or design, the revolver he thrust forward to point at the trio of men smashed through the window to shower shards of glass onto the yard outside.

This as the grim-faced Logan answered Morrow by clawing the fancy revolver from his holster and drawing an unsteady bead on the backs of the three men who suddenly jerked their hands into the air, fingers clawed as if seeking to fasten on something tangible.

"You can't!" Morrow rasped, his voice still sounding helpless after he had made his decision and now lunged to put it into effect. But before he could bring his upraised hand down across the wrist of Logan's gun hand, the stranger had taken more drastic action. And the rancher was unconscious, the shiny revolver slipping from his fingers as his legs buckled. His clear and bright eyes had already rolled up and a dark, slick patch of blood was growing in the white hair at his temples before he crumpled to the ground.

There was time for the Loganville lawman to catch just a glimpse of the impassive face of the stranger before other guns loosed a barrage of fire. Horace Quigley wrenched his gaze away from the tumbling forms along the trail to stare morbidly at the collapsing Logan, then at Edge.

"I sure wouldn't like to have my feet in your shoes when he wakes up, stranger!" he roared.

Edge slid the revolver back into the holster as he murmured inaudibly: "Better than having the head under his hat, feller."

Chapter Seven

IN THE main classroom of the schoolhouse Pierce Starky kicked the entrance door closed with so much force that he stubbed his toe through the leather of his boot and cursed. Then he roared into the bedlam of gunfire and shrieking: "Quit it, Animal! For frig sake, cut it out!"

But his commands failed to penetrate the fat and ugly little man's euphoria. Nevertheless, Animal was able to realize that his six-gun was empty and to recall that he had another fully loaded. He thrust one revolver into the holster and was clawing the second clear when Starky got a grip on him.

"Quit it, I told you!" the taller, older man snarled as he took hold of Animal by the scruff of his neck, yanked him away from the wall, and sent him crashing into desks and chairs.

"You bastard!" Animal raged as the children screamed

and sprang out from behind their desks and Arlene Heller strugged to tear herself free of Benedict Ives.

"Watch out, Pierce!" Ives thundered, and cursed as the woman twisted free of him. He thrust out a foot and she pitched to the floor. "Don't be crazy, Animal!" he shouted as the woman shrieked in alarm and then cried out in pain. She lay on the floor and he pressed a foot into the small of her back to hold her there while the four children yelled at him and tried to drag his foot away from their helpless teacher.

Animal had remained seated on the floor amid the overturned and broken desks and chairs and scattered books and paper. He had kept hold of his revolver but was too enraged by what Starky had done to him to maintain a steady aim. He needed to grip his gun with both hands and bring up his knees to rest his wrists on. By the time he did this, the man with the bushy red mustache and the protruding teeth had gotten one of his guns clear of the holster and was aiming it.

"You do, and I'll kill you for sure!" Ives warned.

Arlene Heller curtailed her struggles and the four children abandoned their efforts to dislodge the man's foot. Starky interrupted his watch through the shattered window and something warned Animal he better shake himself free of the compulsion to make Pierce Starky pay for what he did to him. For stretched seconds after Ives had spoken, everyone in the softly moonlit classroom knew that it was Animal who was under threat and the silence remained absolute.

Until: "You killed him, you killed him," Arlene Heller moaned, her jaw swollen from where Ives had struck her.

Emily Dyer and Lauren Bass began to weep.

Kent Logan challenged: "You wait until my father . . ." but his bravado ran out and he began to tremble.

Marvin James, who was a lot better dressed than his grandfather and displayed a more striking resemblance to old Ira Kyne than did his three siblings, began to curse quietly as he looked around at the man.

Then Starky snarled: "Shut your friggin' mouths, all of you! Animal, cover that back like I already told you once! Ives, stomp her real good if she or any of them goddamn small fry give you any more trouble!"

His voice had power without volume. After he had returned to the glassless window, he smiled in satisfaction and pride at the effect his forceful words had had on his partners and the hostages. There was no talk and all other sounds were held to the minimum as Animal rose gingerly to his feet and went to a rear window and the teacher and students got up off the floor in compliance with the gestures of Ives.

Rod Potts was cleanly dead from the second shot that Starky had fired out of the schoolhouse doorway. He had taken the bullet in the heart. His brother, numbed by grief, went out to get his body. Abner Coburn gave him a hand, the both of them dragging their burden and staying down behind the schoolyard wall for cover. Then, silently but insistently, Glen Potts demanded to continue on his own and carried his brother in both arms into town and along Main Street.

The three men whose sudden appearance on the trail had triggered Animal's hysterical response had not advanced as far as the corner of the walled yard when the shooting started and they went to the ground. Mort Bass lay dead from one bullet in the brain and a second in his throat. Ira Kyne was slightly injured by the shot that took him high in his skinny left arm, but much more seriously hurt by the one that tunneled into his belly. Sam Dyer was unscathed and able to give Edge a hand with carrying the unconscious old man while Coburn and Morrow toted the dungaree-clad corpse.

"I'm sorry, Mrs. Bass," the lawman consoled. The dumpy and dowdy woman was unable to accept this fresh assault on her emotions. She gaped and shrieked in unreasoning denial, then fainted before her nerve finally snapped. Her anxious neighbor was able to catch her crumpling form and lower her gently to the ground.

"Rod said he was gonna try somethin' to rescue Arlene," Ansel Twist admitted wretchedly from the sidewalk out front of Horace Quigley's bullet-shattered store. "But he didn't say what and he said he'd beat me to a pulp if I—"

"Quit whining and lend a hand here, boy! Morrow snapped as he signaled to the liveryman to lower the body of Bass to the ground.

The blacksmith and Edge had already put down the blood-sodden but still breathing burden of the old-timer. The half-breed suggested as the youngster advanced to do the sheriff's bidding: "Figure the best thing you can do, kid, is go bring the local doctor here. We could already have moved him too far with that slug in his belly."

"Yessir!" Twist liked this suggestion better than the sheriff's order. But then he groaned in disappointment as he spotted the rotund figure of Doc Corrigan among the group of a dozen or so Loganville citizens who were hurrying along Main Street in response to the latest barrage of gunfire from the schoolhouse. "Comin' now, sir," Twist reported dully.

"God, did Mr. Logan get hit too, way back here?" the red-haired Coburn asked, his freckled face showing shock as he gasped at the sight of the stylishly garbed rancher sprawled in the hardening mud of the street.

"Stranger smacked him on the head with his six-gun, Abner," Horace Quigley supplied enthusiastically.

"Before I had the chance to grab Mr. Logan's gun," Morrow qualified quickly as the newcomers joined the group encircling the four forms sprawled on the ground— two of them unconscious, one dead, and one perhaps dying. But until the sheriff spoke, most attention had been focused upon the impassive, unshaven, and travel-stained face of Edge. And then as angry eyes shifted from the half-breed, the lawman made himself the focal point of shocked stares and disbelieving glares when he added: "Somebody had to do something to keep him from killing you, Sam. Or Mort. Or Ira."

Incredulity and amazement were now given voice. But the clamour of competing words was, not for the first time that afternoon and evening, curtailed by the strident tones of Pierce Starky.

"All right, you hicks out there! Reckon you've had long enough to count your dead and get your wounded back where you can start patchin' the bastards up! You try some fool thing like that again and—"

"My God, the kids and the teacher," Morrow rasped as the top man of the trio of gunmen began to get into his stride. Then his blue eyes filled with anguish as he

91

whirled to face the cottonwood grove and made a bull-horn of both his hands. "Mister . . . are those four children and the teacher unharmed?"

"Speak when you're friggin' spoken to, punk!" Starky bellowed back.

"That's tellin' the sonofabitch, Pierce!" Animal yelled excitedly.

"This is Sheriff Richard J. Morrow and I'm warning you men!" the lawman continued with less heat but greater determination. "You either give me an assurance that the hostages are all unharmed or I'm about to order an attack . . . and if you three men don't die—"

"So friggin' cut the cackel and come in shootin', asshole!" Benedict Ives challenged.

Another man in the schoolhouse said something in low tones. Then Starky allowed in a more moderate voice than before: "Ain't none of the brats got so much as a scratch or a bruise, punk! The schoolma'am tried to make a run for it and tripped and banged herself up a little is all!"

"To tell Rod to go—" Arlene Heller started to explain, then was hit again and cried out in pain.

"Course, if the stupid cow won't keep quiet like she's been told, Ives here is gonna have to keep on teachin' the teacher—the hard way!" Starky led the raucous laughter at his own joke. Then ended it with a snarled command to his partners and directed his voice out of the shattered window again. "Like I was telling you, you punk hick-town sheriff, no more friggin' tricks!"

"It was not a trick!" Morrow countered, no longer with hands cupped around his mouth. "I didn't authorize what happened! The man who came down off the rise was a friend of Miss Heller! The other three were kin of the children you're holding! They wanted to make the same deal! None of them were armed!''

There was some more rapid whispering in the schoolhouse and some of it sounded like the woman or the children. But no more blows were heard to be struck.

"Punk?" Starky called a few moments later.

"The name's Sheriff Morrow!"

"The teacher and brats want to know the body count!"

"Ain't none of them going to die of what ails them, feller!" the half-breed called before the lawman had time to respond.

"That ain't Morrow!" Starky countered, sounding perturbed, then added: "Doctor, maybe?"

"Just a stranger who knows about gunshot wounds, feller!" Edge answered as everyone in the now enlarged group eyed him quizzically or with suspicion.

There was a short pause, then: "The woman and brats are grateful for the information, punk!"

"Edge!"

"What?"

"That's my name—Edge!"

"Big deal! But the only guy I wanna know out there is the local big shot . . . what's he call himself, Morrow?"

"Logan!" the sheriff bellowed, desperate to beat Edge to the response. As he spoke the name of the rancher who was sprawled unconscious on the ground, the lawman hauled his big Walker Colt from the holster and aimed it from the hip at the abruptly tense half-breed. There was manifest willingness to shoot gleaming in the blue eyes of the man with the leveled gun as he locked his gaze on the glittering stare of his potential victim and thumbed back the hammer. "He's got a big spread and he could be anywhere on it! I already told you men you'll be the first to know when he's located and brought here!"

"We better be, punk! And he better tell you to let us have what we want so we can get the hell away from this hick town!"

There was a note of finality in the man's voice. In the silence that lengthened after this implied threat, there was a lessening of tension among some of those who watched their lawman and the stranger seemingly trying to outstare each other. For despite his bluster, Starky was obviously prepared to wait for Spiro Logan's ruling.

"We're buying time, Mr. . . . Edge," Morrow explained, aware that there was no easing of tension within the man he had drawn his gun against. "I didn't want you yelling anything to those killers without knowing—"

"I get the drift, feller. So, no sweat—long as you put up the gun now."

Morrow, who since the start of the schoolhouse siege had looked all of his age and more, now appeared to his fellow citizens to be shockingly unsure of himself. He gulped and grimaced like a man in pain. But his aim with the big handgun remained rock steady, until Patsy Blair announced her presence in the group.

"Once he's told somebody not to point a gun at him, Rich, he kills them if they do," the bottle-blond, full-bodied music teacher explained evenly. "Looking at him, I see no reason to figure he's all talk. Do figure, though, it made sense for him to say nobody was badly hurt or killed just now. On account of Arlene Heller and the little ones with her have enough on their plates without—"

"There's no arguing with that, Rich Morrow!" Doc Corrigan snapped, and hurried forward to drop to his haunches beside Ira Kyne and feel for a pulse in the scrawny neck of the old man. "Since your ploy has apparently won some time, I suggest we put some of it to good use by removing the injured to where I can make them comfortable."

The gray-bearded Elmo Rankinn elbowed a way out of the press of people and saw with the eye of long experience that one of the prostrated forms in the hardening mud was a corpse. He growled: "And the dead got to be attended to as well, Rich. Only one at my parlor is the ranch hand took there by his brother. Unless you let my two boys out of your posse, I'm gonna need a hand from somebody else with Mort Bass here and Leroy and—"

"Sure, Doc," Morrow allowed. "Okay, Elmo."

He had not looked back at Edge after Patsy Blair began to speak. And his gun hand had gradually inched lower and lower as she and then the doctor and the undertaker said their pieces—each of them drawing nods of agreement from their fellow citizens. Now, as he assigned men to help Corrigan and Rankinn and ordered Abner Coburn to return to his watching post at the front of the schoolhouse, the sheriff eased the big revolver back in his holster. His self-assurance had begun to mount the moment his fellow citizens complied with what he wanted of them, and although he continued to look at least his true age of fifty eight as he returned his attention to Edge, he had a tight control on his anxieties again.

"Appreciate why you lied for the sake of the woman and the children, Edge. Maybe I wouldn't have thought of that. But it doesn't alter how I feel about having your kind in my town."

"You shouldn't judge people by appearances, Rich," Patsy Blair advised.

She was the only one who heard Morrow's words to Edge. Everyone else had moved away, doing as they were asked or drifting back into Loganville of their own free will.

"I hear there's a whole mess of things you shouldn't be doing, Mrs. Blair," the lawman replied sardonically, without a glance at the woman as he swung away from Edge to start toward the cottonwood grove.

For a few moments she struggled against a flare of temper, beat the urge to snarl a retort, and instead muttered bitterly: "Mess is right." Then a look of tenderness spread across her once pretty face as she watched the tall and lean man merge with the shadows of the trees. "Once I had high hopes of that man, mister."

Edge dropped his cigarette butt into a footprint filled with muddy water and asked: "The hotel or the saloon the best place to stay in this town, lady?"

"Neither of them. My place is the best—the music-teaching business isn't booming right now and I could use—"

"Obliged," he told her as he turned and moved back toward the line of stores with a sidewalk fronting them, "but I don't mess with a mess."

"Bastard," she rasped as she followed him up off the drying mud and onto the hollow-sounding boarding, where Horace Quigley was clearing up the bullet-shattered glass of his display window. "You too!" she flung at the store keeper. "All men are bastards!"

She jerked up the hem of her skirts and broke into a run, brushing past the half-breed, the clacking of her feet on the sidewalk perhaps masking the sounds of her weeping.

"Well, I'll be . . . what brought that on, Mr. Edge?" the elderly Loganville rumor monger asked.

"Seems I struck a wrong note with the town music teacher, feller."

Chapter Eight

JUST A handful of Loganville's citizens were still out on the town's two streets to see the running and perhaps crying woman reach the intersection and turn the corner. None of them showed more than fleeting interest in the distraught Patsy Blair after realizing who she was; they simply continued on their way to the Cottonwood Saloon, in haste themselves, but not running. Some of them looked surreptitiously in every direction, as if they felt there was something wrong about what they were doing and were wary of being seen by reproachful eyes.

By the time Edge reached the intersection he was the only figure on either Main Street or River Road. Many men and women, familiar and unfamiliar to him, hurried on by as he had ambled along the western stretch of Main, some of them obviously aware of what was to take place in the saloon. Nobody was turned away from the batwinged entrance, and soon aromatic tobacco smoke, the rise and fall of conversation, and the occasional clink of glass on glass emanated from the Cottonwood—the kind of noises that emanate from any well-patronized saloon in any quiet town where there was little else in the way of entertainment.

"Hey, mister!" Gideon Doyle called from out of his cell. "You saw Sheriff Morrow down the street, I guess?"

"Yeah, feller," Edge answered, not failing to note that the Negro spoke of the lawman with greater respect now.

"Don't guess he made any mention of stoppin' by this place and turnin' me loose now that I almost served my time?" Doyle sounded heavy-hearted, this false front of high spirits gone.

In the saloon, somebody banged something heavy against a hard surface and the muted babble of voices was silenced so that of Sam Dyer could be heard.

"All right now. You all know me and you know I ain't used to standin' up in front of this many people and speakin' my mind. But my little Emily ain't never been in the clutches of no cornered killers before."

"Sam, I don't reckon you oughta—" a woman started to entreat. And before another burst of hammering—maybe a revolver butt on a tabletop—silenced her, Edge recognized the voice of Clara Wade, who had taken his order at the grocery store.

The half-breed was at this time three-quarters of the way across the intersection toward the law office and jailhouse. In the wake of the hammering, another familiar voice came out of the saloon amid the drifting tobacco smoke.

"This ain't no debate around the cracker barrel in Mr. Wade's grocery, Mrs. Wade! My brother's dead. So's Mr. Bass and maybe old man Kyne is by now. And there's those four kids and the schoolteacher—"

"All right, Potts," Dyer said as the voice of the ranch hand began to crack. "And let's not forget those three killers also shot down Leroy Albertson and the two ladies who worked for him at the bank. All right, like the man says, this ain't gonna be no tossin'-ideas-back-and-forth type of meetin'. And since ain't nobody here don't know the situation like it stands, I reckon I'll just put to you what it is you're votin' on."

The law-office door was not locked. It opened soundlessly and closed firmly after Edge had entered, blocking out the noises of the saloon. Enough moonlight filtered through the half-curtained windows for the half-breed to see the layout of the spartanly furnished room.

"Figure you've been in here often enough to know where Morrow keeps the keys to the cells, feller?" he asked through the doorless, square-cornered arch in a side wall.

"Top drawer of the desk, mister," Doyle replied, surprised and a little anxious. He waited until he heard the keys rattling in Edge's hand before he asked: "Hey, Sheriff Morrow tell you to turn me loose but didn't say where he kept the keys?"

There were three cells at the front and three at the rear, with an aisle between. Just the center cell of each three had a window. In the moonlight Edge saw that all the interior walls of the jailhouse were comprised solely of bars, and that each cell was furnished with a narrow cot and a bucket. There was a thin mattress and a blanket on each cot. What was in the bucket in the occupied cell caused Edge to be glad that the second key he tried turned the lock, so he could go back out to the office quickly. From here he replied to Doyle, who had made no move to step away from the window and clear of the cell.

"Morrow made no mention of you, feller. Has his hands full with other things. I'm trusting you to have told the truth when you said you were due for release. If you're lying, then the sheriff is sure going to be mad at me. But how I'll feel toward you—"

"Hey, mister, I wasn't tellin' you no lies! But if Mr. Morrow didn't say for you to turn me loose, then I reckon I'd just as soon stay right here until he comes by and does give the word. If that's all right with you, mister."

"Suit yourself," Edge answered as he eased himself down into the padded armchair behind the uncluttered desk. "Long as you feel free to talk."

"Mister, I ain't never slow to do that and—"

"I noticed. What do you know about the fellers down at the schoolhouse, Doyle?"

"Uh. Well, mister. Like I say, I feel free to talk. But that don't have to mean I'm gonna talk for free . . . if you see what I mean?"

"You hear good, Doyle?"

"Uh? Yeah, ain't nothin' wrong with my ears, mister."

"So listen," Edge told him, and drew the Frontier Colt from his holster, rested the butt on the desk top, and pulled back the hammer. "You hear that?" he asked after a full second of silence.

"I heard it, but I ain't sure I know what it was, sir," the Negro answered nervously.

"Cocked my revolver, Doyle. Whatever you figure your life is worth is how much you're getting for talking to me."

The Negro swallowed noisily and rasped a few low-toned words that could have been an imprecation or a supplication. Then, as Edge set his cocked revolver down on the desk top and leaned back in the comfortable chair, the black man in the cell raised his voice to plead: "Only one I recognized was the one that's called Animal, mister. I served some time with him in a prison up in Omaha. I got drunk that time too. On account of I was gonna marry this real pretty little gal . . . did I tell you the reason I got drunk this time was that me and Betsy Blake—that's the washwoman lives out River Road across from the hog farm . . ." He uttered an annoyed grunt. "But you don't want to hear none of that, Mr.—say what is your name, sir?"

"Edge. And it's getting so that I'm maybe not sure I'm pleased to meet you, Doyle."

"Okay, okay. But I just don't want you to think I'm always gettin' liquored up for no good reason like that Nate Carlin. But anyways, Mr. Edge, I got myself really drunk in Omaha and I socked a lawman who was arrestin' me and that got me a whole thirty days in the hoosegow. And shared a cell with that guy that's called Animal. Called that on account of he's spent so long behind bars, he says. But he's a wild man, right enough. Ain't fifty-two cards to his deck and liable to blow his stack easy as winkin'. He was in that cell at Omaha for train robbery and killin'. Bunch of guys pulled the job

103

and he was the only one to get collared. They was gonna hang him, but he didn't give a shit about that. Had this real strong belief that his partners would get him loose before the rope went around his neck. Believed that like a preacher has faith in the Lord. And they did bust him out, Mr. Edge—the night before the mornin' he was gonna get hung. He always said they'd do that as a kind of joke . . . leave it to the last minute almost. He laughed about it a lot. And I was the only other prisoner that used to laugh along with him when he thought somethin' real strange like that was funny. Reason he took a likin' to me, I guess.''

"The two fellers who rode into town with him today weren't the ones who—''

"Couldn't be, Mr. Edge. On account of how the joke ended, which makes it plain why Animal laughed so much about it. See, soon as one of them that busted him loose—there was three of them—soon as one give him a gun, he shot all of them. Stone dead. Laughin' all the time he was pumpin' bullets into them. Then you know what he done, sir?''

After his timorous start, Gideon Doyle now seemed to be enjoying his account of his association with Animal. He had even moved out of his cell and advanced to the threshold of the law office, where his teeth and the whites of his eyes were starkly visible against the ebony of his skin. "Was only in Omaha once. Never got jailed for what I did there.''

The black man's excitement at his recollections was unaffected by the half-breed's wry lack of enthusiasm. ''The turnkey was only winged—shot in the knee. When he saw what Animal had done to the men that busted him out, the turnkey said Animal was well named. The kind that bit the hand that feeds it. And Animal bit two of that guy's fingers off at the knuckles, Mr. Edge. Both at once, with the one bite. And spit them out into his face. Some Animal, huh? You can see why I warned Mr. Morrow that the town was likely in for trouble when I seen him ride in. Course, the point of that joke was that the turnkey used to bring us our food so it really *was* the hand that—''

"Yeah, feller. Anyone rubs this Animal the wrong way is liable to wind up real hard bitten.''

There was a short pause, then Doyle vented a gust of belly laughter and did some more thigh slapping. Then said amid less obtrusive sounds of glee: "Hey, Mr. Edge, he'd really appreciate that.'' Now the black man became anxiously serious. "Although I hope you ain't askin' me about him because you figure I might be able to get close enough to him to say somethin' to him? That wouldn't be no joke, no sir, it sure wouldn't.''

"You didn't break out with him?''

"No. Oh, he said I could if I wanted. Wouldn't turn loose anyone else in there because they never had laughed along with him. Oh, he liked me well enough, Mr. Edge. But I only had two more days left to serve and I didn't want to get myself wanted for breakin' out of prison that way. He called me a crazy nigger and meant it. And if we had any kind of friendship, I figure it ended right there and then when I wouldn't do what he said I should. He's that kinda wild man, Mr. Edge.''

"The man who's telling him what to do right now is named Pierce Starky?''

"I never heard of him, sir. But ain't no reason why I

should because I ain't no out-and-out criminal that associ—''

''Third man's name is Ives, feller.''

''Benedict Ives?'' Doyle asked in a strangled tone as a burst of loud talk from the saloon reached into the law office by the way of the barred window in the cell the black man had recently occupied. There was an element of contentiousness in the din that was then abruptly curtailed by the hammering of the improvised gavel. ''Man, oh man. I sure enough have heard of him. Never did get to see him, though.''

''Out of the same mold as the one called Animal?''

''No, sir . . . well, maybe he kills easy as Animal does and without no pity for them that dies. But he don't kill just for the hell of it the way Animal is likely to do. Woman is what makes that Benedict Ives so twisted up and mean, Mr. Edge. He has to have them like other men gotta have liquor or tobacco. And like we all gotta have food and water. Them that he gets easy—whores, mostly, I guess—he don't treat so well. Them that he takes by force—well, all I heard is stories. That he cuts them open, slices pieces off them, scalps them, and stuff like that. It's said that one time he—''

''I've got the picture, feller,'' Edge cut in as he rose from the chair and picked up his Colt; eased the hammer forward before he slid the revolver back in the holster.

''Tell me something now, Mr. Edge?'' Doyle asked as he watched the half-breed move to one of the half-curtained windows.

''I've got the time,'' was the even-toned reply. ''Inclination depends on what you want to know.''

He took out the makings as he watched three men emerge from the Cottonwood and turn east along Main Street.

"Why is a man like you concerned with Loganville trouble, Mr. Edge?"

"Man like me?" the half-breed countered as he watched Glen Potts, Sam Dyer, and Ansel Twist step down off the saloon stoop and angle across the street, away from the line of houses that Spiro Logan rented to the family men he employed at his Meadowlark spread. Then the trio disappeared.

"Well . . . no offense intended, sir. But the way I seen you handle yourself and scare the shit outta Nate Carlin when him and Patsy Blair tried what they did . . . well, sir, I'd say the style of trouble you go lookin' for is in a bigger—"

Edge had struck a match on the butt of his Colt and now held the flame just a half inch away from the fresh-rolled cigarette at the side of his mouth. His eyes glittered and his teeth were displayed in a silent snarl he could see reflected in the window.

"I say somethin', sir?" Doyle asked anxiously after another loud gulp.

"I never go looking for anything of the kind, feller," the half-breed replied, and now lit the cigarette, shook out the match, and dropped it to the floor.

"Yeah . . . yessir, I know how that can be. Any man with a black skin in a white folks' world will know what you mean. Like I said, no offense?"

"No sweat. I don't usually butt in on business that's no concern of mine, Doyle. Just went down the street to order some supplies and see to it that the saloon keeper and liveryman knew where to find the money I'd left for them. All I got done was placing my order at the grocery. After that, I got to seeing how close the sheriff is to cracking under the strain of what's happening here. And the rest of the people didn't look to be in such good shape to do something if he let them down.''

He leaned closer to the window to peer out across the intersection—saw that the faces that had been at the windows of the saloon were now gone. There was a larger press of people at the entrance of the Cottonwood, though, but nobody was yet ready to push out through the batwings.

''Well, sir, Mr. Morrow, he ain't—''

Edge straightened up and blew a stream of smoke at the pane, where it hit and spread in all directions. After it had disintegrated he could see the reflection of Gideon Doyle behind him. The image was indistinct, but the sniff as the black man sought to relish the tobacco smoke at second hand was very clear.

''The lawman's nothing to me and I don't owe anybody else in this town anything, feller,'' the unusually voluble half-breed went on. ''The schoolteacher included. But I figure everyone owes something to kids. Even those who didn't have anything to do with bringing them into the world.''

Gideon Doyle allowed a long pause to develop—was uneasy with the silence that did not seem to bother Edge but reluctant to say anything in case the white man was not yet finished. Then he assayed: ''Miss Heller could be gettin' a hard time from Ives. And if any of the little ones are girls . . . well, maybe that twisted—''

"Two girls. And there's no need to say anything else about him."

"Whatever you want. You ain't got any makin's to spare, have you?"

"No, none to spare."

"Sure. Sure. Hey, mister, I ain't surprised that Rich Morrow is lettin' this thing get on top of him. He's got a fine reputation around here and is real highly thought of by most everybody. Them that ain't been around the country some, like me, anyway. And them that turn a blind eye to troubles that happen a long ways from here and make out like they ain't happenin'. Way it can be in a quiet and law-abidin' town like Loganville where nothin' bad ever happens—or didn't until today.

"Take that itsy-bitsy branch of the bank that got robbed. Seems there's been talk about puttin' in bars and a vault and stuff like that for ages. But never was done on account of it never was figured anybody'd plan on hittin' the place. Yessir, that Rich Morrow had himself a reputation for runnin' a law-abidin' town that nobody could fault, I reckon. On account of nobody broke the law. A local ordinance now and then, maybe. But that was all."

He paused to sniff in some more of Edge's expelled smoke. Then the silence quickly unnerved him again and he continued with his talking for the sake of filling it.

"Stands to reason the sheriff is just bound to be shakin' all over inside of him on account of this real bad trouble. Why, the biggest worry that he's ever had before in Loganville was when that Patsy Blair come to town and set her cap at him. She was a real beauty back then . . . two years ago it was, a couple of months after I got here. Mr. Morrow, he fell for her real hard and she didn't give him any reason to think he wasn't the only one—that he could see, anyways. But a whole lot of other men were payin' calls at the Widow Blair's house and it wasn't no piano learnin' they was getting in the back room.

"Local law against there bein' any whorin' in Loganville and there ain't many who wouldn't say Patsy Blair didn't break that law a whole lot of times. Never did serve any time for it, though, after Mr. Morrow found out what was goin' on. Most of the time, the sheriff he just pretends like she ain't around. Which don't sit too well with her. Regrets not ropin' and brandin' him when she had him eatin' outta the palm of her hand is how folks hereabouts figure it. And she sure let herself go so she ain't no beauty no more, mister. Not so many local men visit with her these days and she's got a real bad mouth when she's crossed. Only one around here that calls me nigger and cusses me off on account of my color and nothin' else. Yessir, the Widow Blair is one lady that ain't no more. And what she is . . . well, Mr. Edge, if she ever gets herself knocked up, I ain't gonna put my name down for one of the pups."

"Obliged for the talk, feller," the half-breed said as he pressed his face close to the window. Then moved to the door after glancing across the intersection as people began to emerge from the Cottonwood Saloon.

"I ain't gonna leave this jailhouse before Mr. Morrow says I can," Doyle said with a tone of complaint as

Edge opened the law-office door but remained on the threshold.

"No sweat," the white man replied to the black as he surveyed the main street of Loganville in both directions. Then tossed his part-smoked cigarette into the mud.

"Shit," Doyle groaned.

"Uh?"

"Since you didn't do me no favor unlockin' the cell door, I was gonna ask if maybe I could have what you didn't smoke."

"A man could catch something off smoking another man's leavings, feller."

"I'd have been ready to risk that, mister," Gideon Doyle countered, raising his voice—in irritation with the intractable man in the doorway and against the mounting volume of noise on the street. "If you knew the kinda stuff I've smoked in bad times . . . wood shavin's, all kindsa tree leaves, dried animal crap, hollow sticks, grass—"

"Sometimes it seems the whole world's going to pot, feller," Edge cut in on the sour-toned black man. "Here."

He had taken the poke from his pocket and half turned to toss this toward the man. Who caught it with a reflex action, grinned, was momentarily anxious that the white man might he playing a trick on him, and then said: "Thanks . . . thanks, mister. I really do appre—"

"Roll just one and I'll be back for the change later."

"This is a real kindness, sir, that a man like me wouldn't never expect from one like you, Mr. Edge!" Doyle called out through the doorway that the half-

111

breed had left open as he stepped off the threshold of the law office.

There was a lot of noise out on the street now—footfalls and the clop of horse hooves and a hum of many voices, all of them anxious but none shouting. Nevertheless, as he dropped gratefully into Morrow's chair behind the desk and began to roll a cigarette, Gideon Doyle clearly heard Edge answer him: "Figure I must have taken a shine to you!"

Chapter Nine

GLEN POTTS, Sam Dyer, and Ansel Twist had left the saloon to go to the livery stable. And now they came back along the street, each leading a saddled horse. If any of the three men was aware of Edge standing out front of the law office, he gave no sign of it. The skinny youngster did direct several uneasy glances toward the large group of people who had come out of the Cottonwood to stand at the point where River Road and Main Street met. The powerfully built blacksmith recognized the youngster's trepidation and rasped something to him out of the corner of his mouth. After which Twist joined Dyer and the ranch hand in peering resolutely the way they were going.

Then, when these three grim-faced men leading the horses by the bridles had crossed the intersection onto the western stretch of the street, the crowd that had been watching from River Road fell in behind them.

Some eagerly and others will ill-concealed misgivings; some obviously as determined as Potts and Dyer to see the plan through while just as many were even more perturbed than Ansel Twist about their involvement. Many of the fifty or more in the group cast glances at the law office. And one man, anonymous in the midst of the press of people, challenged: "Stay outta this business, stranger!"

He was scolded into silence by many voices and then the familiar voice of Clara Wade yelled from within the saloon: "Reckon he's got more sense than to fool with this tomfoolery!"

Several members of the losing minority, who remained in the Cottonwood after the vote, grunted in agreement.

Edge spit into the drying mud as he moved unhurriedly after the Loganville citizens who were determined to bring matters to a head. His spitting could have been a response to either or both comments—or merely an attempt to rid his mouth of a bad taste.

As the people advanced closer to the end of the street, they closed up into a more tightly knit group behind the men with the horses, as if they were becoming more uneasy with every step and sought to draw comfort from proximity with others of like mind. On past the meeting hall, the funeral parlor, and the barbershop, bank and church in the graveyard—the bank, where the tragic events had started, now dark. All the stores across the street were also dark. But there were lights burning behind the draped windows of Doc Corrigan's office. And, abruptly, a bright wedge of lamplight was thrown out across the sidewalk as the office door was pulled open after the tight formed body of men and women had past by—and the broadly built form of Spiro Logan stepped over the threshold.

The rancher's dude Western outfit was missing the Stetson now, but he had his fancy revolver back in the holster. His wound was no longer seeping blood but the whiteness of his hair at the temple was still marred by discoloration. From the way he glared across the street at Edge, it was plain Logan had been told who crashed a gun barrel into his head. He snarled at the half-breed as another man yelled harsh words to draw his attention.

"What the hell is it you people have in mind to do?"

It was Sheriff Morrow who made the demand as he emerged from the timber that partly obscured the schoolhouse, and came to a halt, arms akimbo, on the moonlit trail midway between the end of the street and the schoolyard wall. No attempt was made to answer the lawman until the deputation of Loganville citizens had come to a halt, those at the front some fifteen feet away from where Morrow stood, the expression on his rugged featured face as inflexible as his stance.

Then, as just Edge on one side and Logan on the other continued to advance, Sam Dyer said adamantly: "We took a democratic vote, Rich. Wasn't no countin' of hands done 'cause there wasn't no need. Clear to see a whole lot more was for givin' the killers what they want than was for doin' it your way." He hooked a thumb and jerked it over his shoulder. "These folks here."

There was some nodding of heads and less than enthusiastic agreement with the grim-faced blacksmith.

"And those that voted against us, Sheriff," Glen

Potts added, ''said they'd stay back at the saloon and not take a hand in . . .'' He shrugged.

''Abide by the democratic decision,'' Dyer said, in the manner of a man reciting by rote something that had taken him a great deal of effort to commit to memory.

''So step aside and let's get this over and done with before anyone else gets killed, Rich Morrow!'' a woman demanded from the center of the crowd.

''Ain't nobody means you no disrespect, Rich,'' Dyer hurried to say. And then a note of pleading for understanding entered his voice. ''No one blames you for nothin'. We was all behind you until Mort and the Potts boy got killed and old Ira was so bad shot up. But since then we—''

''Potts and you others who tried to make a deal with those killers . . .'' the hard-faced Morrow started to argue. But his voice trailed away as he saw that Edge was closing with him from the right and Spiro Logan from the left. ''What the—''

''I'm with the sheriff, stranger!'' the rancher rasped through his very white, gritted teeth. He raised and curled his right hand so that it was close to touching his holstered revolver.

''Draw that pretty Remington against me, feller, and you'll be with the rest of the corpses down at the undertakers,'' the half-breed countered as he halted on one side of Morrow at the same time as Logan aligned himself with the lawman on the other side.

The rancher caught his breath.

Morrow scowled and regained his composure. ''Appreciate your support, Mr. Logan. But I don't need the help of any tough-talking fast gun looking to profit from this town's trouble." He looked at neither of the men who flanked him as he spoke to them in turn but kept a wary eye on the crowd who had voted to take a stand against him. Now, in an almost cajoling tone, he urged them: "Go on back to the saloon or your homes and allow me and the posse of deputies I swore in to deal with—"

"Edge, is that your name?" Glen Potts asked with an insistence that seemed to grind the lawman into silence. He was a good-looking man of twenty-five or six with a weathered and tough-looking face. Now his flesh was pale and he looked vulnerable, as if somehow grief for his brother had caused him to shrink so that his workaday clothing no longer fit his once muscular frame.

"Potts, I know how you must feel about your—" Spiro Logan started, but broke off at a signal from Morrow.

"Edge is right, feller."

"Ranch work don't pay high. But I had some savin's that were in Mr. Albertson's bank. Same as Rod did. Ready to give you all of it if you'll lend me a hand to go get the killers after they take off from the school."

"Young man, our first priority is to get the children out of danger and—" a woman Edge thought was Mrs. Sullivan reminded harshly.

"I'm not in the bounty-hunting business right now," the half-breed cut in on her to tell Glen Potts.

"Son, stranger," Sam Dyer said dully, shifting his lackluster gaze from one to the other. "What that lady just said is surely right and it's my intention to do that." He looked over one shoulder, then the other as he challenged. "And if you folks ain't willin' to back me up just because Rich Morrow has got some extra help, then . . . well, I'm real sorry I ever thought of you as good friends and neighbors.''

He started forward then, tugging on the bridle of his horse. Ansel Twist followed a moment later, then Glen Potts. The ranch hand had looked hard at Edge, as if seeking to read some message behind the half-breed's impassive face. And the townspeople shuffled into movement behind the leading trio of men.

''Sheriff?'' Logan rasped anxiously from the side of his mouth.

Morrow uttered an obscenity that was no louder than the rancher's plea.

Edge drawled: ''Get rid of the gun, feller.''

The soft-spoken command brought the group to another halt and there was a tense silence that lasted for perhaps two full seconds before Potts spoke. ''I ain't no gunslinger like you, mister, but if you wanna take my gun off me, you'll have to kill me first and—''

''You show yourself to those killers in the schoolhouse with that six-shooter on your hip and—'' The half-breed was interrupted by the blacksmith.

''Sonofabitch,'' Dyer groaned, anguish displacing the composure he had been straining to maintain. ''I didn't think about that pistol of yours, Potts. The man's right. Get rid of the gun belt, son.'' He looked over his shoulder at the tense faces of his supporters, all of them wan in the moonlight. ''And anyone else who's armed— either get rid of your weapons or stay back from the schoolhouse.''

Just for a moment the grief-stricken vengeful Glen Potts nurtured his resentment for Edge. But then he rapidly unbuckled his gun belt as mumbling talk rose and fell behind him—everyone assuring the blacksmith and their other fellow citizens that they carried no weapons.

"I'll take it, Glen," the white-haired and bright-eyed rancher offered in a solicitous tone, extending a hand toward Potts.

"You already got one gun, Mr. Logan!" Sam Dyer rasped angrily. Then his tone was calm as he added: "And I hear you were ready to use that on the backs of some of us the last time we tried to get the children—"

"I was going to call on you to halt, that's all!" Spiro Logan retorted with rising anger of his own. And there was a dangerous glitter in his eyes and a menacing tenseness in his stance as he watched Dyer take the gun belt from the unresisting Potts and toss it toward Morrow.

The rancher opened his mouth to speak but there was a disturbance in the crowd and Emily Bass emerged to demand caustically: "When you people are through passin' the time of day with each other, I'd like to remind you there's children's lives in danger in this town tonight!"

Certainly the ashen-faced, red-eyed, woman spoke in louder tones than had anyone else since Morrow halted the mass advance on the schoolhouse. And perhaps her voice was the only one to carry clearly through the moon-shadowed cottonwoods to the captors and captives in the school.

Pierce Starky yelled: "That's friggin' right, lady! Time for talkin' is through! Me and my partners don't get the horses right now, we start shootin'! And 'cause we like little kids as much as much as anyone else . . . well, almost, the teacher'll get it first!''

"Oh, no," Ansel Twist groaned, and this time it was the skinny youngster who was first to move.

"We're bringin' them now, mister!" Sam Dyer roared, tugging a horse into motion.

And then, as Emily Bass hurried to take the lead, the entire crowd surged forward to bear down on Edge and Morrow and Logan. Who stood their ground on the center of the trail impassively, reproachfully, and angrily so that the mass of resolute people had to divide and then reform again after swinging to either side of the unyielding line.

"If my boy gets hurt because you let them try this, Morrow . . ." Logan started to rasp, but lost the thread of the threat as all three men turned to face the rear of the crowd.

"You'd have me shoot those people down when maybe they're doing the right thing, Mr. Logan?" the lawman countered bitterly, then added with a shake of his head: "And when I don't know any other way to handle it?"

"What about you, hard man?" the dudishly garbed rancher growled. And his attempt to stoke the fires of anger was again foiled by a more urgent demand upon his emotions. And he challenged in a strangely cracked tone of voice: "If you can bring this trouble to an end without anyone else getting hurt, Edge, I can afford one hell of a lot more money than Potts."

"I just know a man who knows a man, feller," the half-breed answered with a glance back along Main Street, which was filling with other people. "There wouldn't have been any charge." Then he glimpsed Gideon Doyle standing outside the law office, a cigarette angled from his lips, and qualified: "By me, anyway."

He returned his glinting eyes to the more than fifty Loganville citizens who were backing the town blacksmith. They had complied with the low-toned instructions of Dyer and spread themselves into a line facing the wall and across the schoolhouse yard. There was no apparent order except that husbands and wives stood shoulder to shoulder in the silent, grim-faced, and motionless row. At the far end, Dyer, Twist, and Potts had positioned themselves and the horses at the gateway in the low wall. After a frantic discussion in tones of muted anger, Emily Bass won the right to speak for the townspeople.

But, after waiting for the men and women to form the line, it was the killers in the schoolhouse who were the first to raise their voices.

"Okay, okay!" Pierce Starky yelled from the broken window of the main classroom. "You got the horses! But what's with all the people you brought?"

"Yeah, there's too many lousy people out there on the trail!" Benedict Ives accused from the cracked-open doorway.

"And we're still surrounded, Pierce!" Animal reminded from deeper inside the building. "I can still see them sneakin' around in the trees out there!"

The short, fat, plain-featured, and shabbily garbed new widow took two full seconds to compose herself before she spoke to the murderers of her husband and

121

captors of her daughter. Then she demanded forcefully: "Thought you men were sick of all the talk?"

"We friggin' are, lady, and—" Starky began to bellow.

"So listen, damn you!" the woman shouted him down. "And let's get this over and done so we can—"

"Mommy?" Lauren Bass shrieked.

The little girl's voice shattered her mother's brittle veneer of self-confidence. "Oh, my God . . . My baby, my baby . . . I'm comin' Lauren!"

Emily Bass had seemed rooted to the spot in the gateway as she responded to her daughter's plea. Then, as if she had been violently shoved in the back, she lunged into the yard.

"Shit!" Sam Dyer snarled, and powered after her.

"Sonofabitch!" Glen Potts roared, and launched himself in the same direction.

He reached the older man in three strides, dove at the woman, and all three of them crashed to the ground.

"God Almighty!" Ansel Twist shrieked, holding the bridle of his horse as he grabbed for the reins of the two animals that had been abandoned.

"Stay back or I'll friggin' kill all of you!" Benedict Ives warned shrilly.

"It's all a lousy stinkin' trick, Pierce!" Animal snarled.

"Get down, get down, get down!" Rich Morrow commanded as he sprang forward. Spiro Logan was quick to follow.

Then everyone except Twist threw themselves to the ground in the cover of the wall. Just a moment before Starky and Ives loosed a fusillade of shots from the doorway and broken window at the front of the schoolhouse. It was impossible to tell from which gun the first bullet was fired, but the shattering of another window a moment or so later indicated that Animal had started to fire on the Rankinn brothers who were in the timber out back.

For several seconds it seemed as if every man, woman, and child in Loganville was shouting curses and pleas to the limits of their vocal capacity. Only moments after Emily Bass lunged toward her daughter, it had been possible to hear snatches of phrases and single words. Now there was only a rising babble of anger. Then the gunfire exploded and for what seemed an eternity the cracking of bullets against stone and timber competed for dominance with the keening shrillness of the voices.

Edge's contribution to the din was a string of vehement curses as he raced off the trail and into the trees on the town side of the grove. Which brought him close enough to Byron Pardo to hear the dentist and veterinarian yell: "I don't believe it! I don't believe none of what's happening here!"

Pardo was a short, fat man of middle age dressed in a city suit and hatless. Despite the chill of the spring night air, beads of sweat stood out on his pale face. He was down on his haunches, his back to the wall and his head tucked below the top of it; a Winchester rested across his thighs. He was dry-washing his hands.

"Kent!" Spiro Logan roared from the trail. "Oh, God! Kent. Kent! Oh, no, pl—" The rancher's voice was driven to a falsetto it was impossible to sustain and he was forced into anguished silence.

And Edge, as he saw what had caused the man's hysterical outburst, dropped down to his haunches, drew

123

his razor from the neck pouch, and leaned close to the terrified Pardo to snarl: "You better believe I'll open you up to see if you bleed yellow—if you don't—"

"Lay off him, stranger!" a man of similar age but bigger build than Pardo roared as he stepped from behind a stout tree trunk, a revolver aimed from his hip. His clothing rather than his breath smelled of liquor, which suggested he was Joseph Snyder who ran the saloon.

"You'll do if he won't, feller," Edge snapped, and used the razor that he had been holding in front of Pardo's mesmerized eyes to point over the wall.

"The bastards!" Snyder snarled, and it was as if this were some prearranged signal that everyone felt bound to obey.

For the shooting and shouting came to abrupt end. Footfalls continued for a few moments longer—people scampering and scurrying along Main Street to get to the scene of the fresh violence. Here and there, a whimper or a curse, a sob or a groan could be heard. Sounds that were somehow eerie and almost unreal in the sudden silence. The new advance on the Loganville schoolhouse lost impetus. As the pace slowed, so did the march of booted feet.

Then all voices were stilled. Except for that of Edge, who pitched his so that it could only be heard by Snyder—and Pardo, who seemed too terrified to hear.

"Cover me," Edge murmured. And thrust the razor back into the pouch as he powered up from the crouch and leaped over the wall.

For a stretched second he was sure that the boy was dead and that he was about to be blasted into the same eternity by the same guns. Kent Logan lay where he had fallen—spread eagled on his back, with dark stains on his shirtfront. In the moonlight that cast no shadow of trees across this area of the schoolyard, it was easy to see that his eyes were closed and his mouth gaped open. There seemed to be not even the slightest movement of his narrow chest to signal that this twelve-year-old boy was still breathing.

Edge had seen Kent Logan plunge through the shattered window of the classroom a second before the boy's father cried out his name. Guns were still directing a hail of bullets out of the window and doorway then and any number of these shots could have blasted into the boy's back. Certainly he staggered as he hit the rain-softened surface of the dirt yard and took just three or four long strides before he pitched to the ground—facedown but then turning so that he rolled over on his back before he became so awesomely inert.

It was probably more than mere coincidence that caused the men in the schoolhouse to hold their fire at the precise moment that the young boy fell. Hardened killers though they obviously were, they had found themselves shocked into rigid inaction by the gunning down of the helpless and terrified boy.

But there was no guarantee that the men trapped in the schoolhouse would remain so for more than a few moments. The half-breed presented a far larger target than the skinny youngster, and he was inviting a barrage of gunfire by seemingly charging toward the killers.

''Get down inside!'' Morrow bellowed, and exploded a shot toward the schoolhouse.

But Snyder or Pardo had fired first, a bullet that

thudded into the timber frame of the broken window. And Edge's scowl became a grin as he whistled between his gritted teeth and dropped his hand away from his holstered Colt and dove to the ground—slithering more than three feet through the mud to push his hands and arms beneath the thighs and shoulder blades of the unmoving boy.

A whole barrage of gunfire was being loosed at the facade of the schoolhouse now. And not for the first time, the half-breed's senses seemed to function with far more effective intensity than was usual. So that as he dragged his knees forward and arched his back, then rose up with the boy held securely in his arms, he knew precisely what was taking place on all sides of him.

He saw muzzle flashes, smelled black powder smoke, heard the cracks of bullets, felt Kent Logan's pulse at his throat, and tasted mud on his own lips.

He ran across the yard with the burden he was sure was alive, heading for the gateway where Sam Dyer was now helping Ansel Twist to calm the shying horses as Glen Potts dragged the violently struggling Emily Bass through the gap and clear of the flailing hooves.

Two guns were blasting at the front of the building from the half-breed's left—a rifle and a revolver—Byron Pardo had been stirred to action. While to the right, Ben Wade and Luke Farris were blazing away with handguns. These men were firing out of deep moon shadow; in the bright daubs of muzzle flashes, they looked like ghosts. Rich Morrow, Spiro Logan, Nathan Carlin, and Abner Coburn were standing on the trail, unevenly spaced out and presenting themselves as clear targets as they sprayed the building with bullets—the liveryman pumping the repeater action of his Winchester while the other three exploded shots from revolvers.

Edge was conscious of bullets that cracked and whined close to his head and also felt the occasional jerk of his sheepskin coat as it was snagged by flying lead. But even with his senses working at such a pitch, he was unable to discern if any of the near misses came from behind him. Until he skidded through the gateway and crashed heavily to the ground—heard a bullet ricochet off the wall and felt chips of stone sting his cheek.

"He hurt bad?" Sam Dyer demanded breathlessly as he and Ansel Twist dropped to the ground after they had abandoned their struggles to calm the spooked horses.

"Town's got a doctor with the time and training I never had," the half-breed rasped. All the shots he now heard came from the schoolhouse; the Loganville citizens had ceased fire.

In the safe cover of the wall, Edge was no longer so highly perceptive about what was happening around him. But he did see Glen Potts and Mrs. Bass stretched out on the trail, the ranch hand no longer needing to restrain the formerly hysterical woman. The mother of the hostage child seemed numb as she stared at the boy who looked dead but was not. Edge also saw the red-haired, freckle-faced Abner Coburn crouched behind the wall a few feet away, as were Carlin, Morrow, and Spiro Logan.

Edge saw these anxiously watching people with just a fleeting glance in the silence after the final shot of the last barrage. And glimpsed too the mass of men and women who had not fallen in with the blacksmith's plan and came late to the end of Main Street.

"He's breathin', Edge, I can see he's breathin'," Potts gasped as the half-breed ran his hands over the frail form of the boy.

"He ain't dead, Mr. Logan!" Ansel Twist yelled, proud to be first to broadcast the good news.

Benedict Ives roared from the classroom: "We don't give a shit about that one brat! We still got us three more and the teacher! And unless you go bring them horses we want, ain't none of them gonna be breathin' much longer! Right, Pierce!"

None of the people crouched or sprawled in the cover of the wall could avoid hearing the threat. But none paid more than passing attention as they gazed with varying degrees of concern at the half-breed, his mouth in a grin that failed to inject any warmth into the glittering slits of his eyes.

"Mud on his shirt and I figure ink on his hands," Edge reported evenly a second or so after Ives had failed to draw a response from Starky.

"Just fainted," Dyer suggested.

"Or knocked himself out when he fell," Edge answered, rising to move away from the group near the gateway.

"Pierce . . . what's wrong, Pierce?" Ives demanded, harsh menace displayed by a shrill tone of fear in his voice.

Spiro Logan, his fine clothes sullied by mud, scampered past the half-breed, obviously wanting to express the gratitude that showed on his pale and drawn face. But whatever first word of thanks was formed in his throat emerged only as a gasping sob. And he did not quite manage to avert his head before the brightness of his eyes gave way to tears that now began to course down his cheeks.

"You people, you lousy, friggin' people!" Starky snarled as Edge reached Nathan Carlin and Rich Morrow.

"He sounds—" the lawman began to blurt with an expression akin to a grin of triumph.

"You shot me!" the leader of the gunmen went on. Growing physically weaker by the moment, the prematurely gray man with the nondescript features was unable to snarl out his words with vehemence now. But it was easier for his unseen audience to hear him. And those who risked showing themselves saw the reason for this apparent paradox—Pierce Starky had emerged from the doorway and now came out from the shadowed porch. He took four unsteady paces across the moon-bright yard and came to a halt, his feet placed far apart as he struggled to remain upright while he clutched at his belly with both hands. Blood oozed from the cracks between his fingers and he swayed. The door behind him remained wide open as he issued the ominous warning: "Are you gonna be friggin' sorry it was me, you . . ."

His voice trailed away and his head dropped forward. His hands clawed and he vented a choked cry of pain. But then he wrenched his chin up off his chest and the grimace on his face became a sneer as he summoned his final reserves of energy to snarl: "They're good as dead! Horses or not, those poor kids and their teacher are gonna be—"

Then he died. On his feet, with the rattle punctuating his unfinished augury and his bloodied hands dropping to his sides as his head fell forward again. A moment later he collapsed hard on to his knees, then tipped away from the rigid vertical and pitched into a face-down sprawl.

"Okay, you deal with me now!" Benedict Ives thundered, and showed himself for just a moment on the threshold of the schoolhouse as he slammed the door closed.

"But don't you pay no mind to what Pierce told you!" Animal made haste to add. "You give us the horses and none of the kids and the teacher neither'll be hurt! Just the two horses we want now!"

The tall and lean Ives had recovered from the impulse to panic when he first realized Starky had been hurt. Now his tone suggested he was not merely in control of himself but was elated to be in control of the schoolhouse, regardless of the circumstance that had given him command. The fat and ugly little man known as Animal, however, sounded like he had been plunged into a blue funk by Starky's death.

"The horses bolted!" Morrow called, remaining in a half crouch so that he was able to keep watching the schoolhouse. "We'll have to go bring them—"

"No, asshole!" Ives cut in, and the force of his words acted like a gunshot—caused Morrow and some of the others at the wall to flinch and even duck their heads down out of sight. "We don't want no nags that've run themselves into the ground! Bring us a couple of fresh mounts, lawman!"

"Whatever you say."

"You better do whatever I say! And do it quick, asshole! I ain't like Pierce Starky! I ain't got no patience! What I do have—me and Animal both—is plenty bullets!

And if we have to kill the brats and the dame, ain't no way you'll take us alive to throw no necktie party for us, lawman!''

"I believe you, Ives! Need to pull back now and fix it for the horses to—"

"Just do it, asshole!''

"Damn you, Rich Morrow!'' Emily Bass snarled as the sheriff and Nathan Carlin began to follow Edge, who had already reached Main Street and was in the cover of the trees.

"Mrs. Bass?'' the lawman asked as he held back from following the scampering Carlin and peered at the woman with shocked eyes.

"You murderin' scum in there?'' she demanded, ignoring the perplexed Morrow.

"You got a bad mouth, lady!'' Ives accused.

"We need to know the children and Arlene Heller are still safe!''

"Oh, hell, I should have . . .'' the sheriff groaned.

"Wasn't us that threw lead around in here, lady!''

"Ives, why keep—'' Animal started, and was halted by the rasping voice of his partner.

"Shit, girl, tell them, I said!''

"We're . . . we're all right, Mrs. Bass,'' the school-teacher called in a strained and tearful voice. "Lauren and Emily and Marvin aren't hurt. Nor me. But please . . . the sooner this can be over . . . I don't know how much more—"

"All right, that's enough!'' Ives snapped. And his voice rose as he turned from the despairing Arlene Heller to command the townspeople: "No argument! Animal got it wrong! Four is how many mounts we want! On account of we're gonna take a couple with us a short ways! A couple of people that is what I mean! Make sure we get clear of this lousy town without us gettin' our—''

Emily Bass, Sam Dyer, Ansel Twist, and Glen Potts began a discordant chorus of objections. And Ives allowed himself to be silenced for perhaps five seconds before he triggered a shot. The teacher screamed and the children began to weep.

''Shut up! Friggin' shut up, all of you!'' Ives thundered, his voice shrill with near-hysterical rage. And then there was another pause, self-imposed, that allowed him to regain his composure before he went on. ''All right, no harm done. Except to the ceilin'. I told you people, no argument. And I don't want so many of you assholes out there when you bring the mounts. Just a couple of men with the animals. And if you don't think I ain't in no position to make sure what I tell you goes . . . well . . . well, you just give me some cause to fire again and prove it. You just do that. All right?''

The close-to-cracking teacher had managed to silence the terrified children, and the people out on the trail were even quieter as, with the exception of Abner Coburn, they began to withdraw.

The liveryman tacitly acknowledged Morrow's signaled instruction to remain where he was near the gateway. Then Spiro Logan came warily to his feet, the still-unconscious boy draped limply in his arms. The rest of those who had been crouched in the cover of the front wall of the schoolyard also rose cautiously, Mrs. Bass stubbornly but noiselessly gesturing that she required no assistance from Sam Dyer or Glen Potts on the short walk back to Main Street.

Fear was almost palpable in the night air as the small group advanced on the large crowd. But nobody submitted to the urge to make a panicked dash for safety. And relief was muted when the immediate danger was over, everyone grimly aware that the lives of three children and their teacher were still on the line in the schoolhouse amid the cottonwoods. Probably, even, the hostages were in greater peril than before. For the warning spoken by the dying Pierce Starky and the deranged manner of Benedict Ives were still terrifyingly fresh in the minds of most Loganville citizens.

As a delayed reaction to this, recriminations began to be voiced. After the guilt-ridden and the afraid had watched Spiro Logan carry his son into the doctor's office, suddenly it seemed as if everyone turned upon everyone else with bitter-toned accusations.

Close to where Edge and Gideon Doyle leaned against the cemetery wall, the stout and homely Olive Carlin sneered at her husband: "Reckon you figured you looked quite the hero?"

"What's that?" the city-suited barber countered absently.

"When Rich Morrow shoved young Potts's gun at you and you started in to shoot at the school. And you was too liquored up to know you could've got yourself killed—at the start, leastways."

"Did my best when I was called on to help my neighbors in a time of trouble," the town drunk answered. He constantly glanced along the street, apparently anxious to return quietly to the Cottonwood for a refill of Dutch courage.

"For *her* to see!" his wife snarled as the half-breed mimed the actions of rolling a cigarette and Gideon Doyle returned his poke to him.

"Who, woman?" Carlin demanded impatiently.

"That woman! That brazen Blair widow that'll go with anythin' in pants!"

"You're . . ." He sighed, squelching a flare of temper, and shook his head as he growled: "Woman, if you had a mind, you'd be out of it."

"Maybe I ain't so bright, Nathan Carlin, but there's not a thing wrong with my hearin' and my eyesight! I heard tell how you drew a gun on that gunfightin' stranger there." She poked an accusing finger at Edge, who appeared to be paying no attention to anything as he carefully rolled a cigarette. "Just to impress that . . . that . . . woman that you was in the saloon alone with! And I see you comin' down the street with her brazen as can be! While *I* was helpin' *my* neighbors! Standin' alongside Sam Dyer and the rest without no guns to defend ourselves with if them killers started in to shoot at us! And where was you when we was all votin' to do that? And where was the Widow Blair? What was you impressin' her with then?"

"You're crazy," her husband accused, having become steadily more composed as she got angrier. Then he swung around and strolled off toward the saloon.

This response acted to confound Olive Carlin, who at once became self-consciously aware that others besides the Negro and the stranger might well have seen and heard her fighting with her husband. Then, as she abashedly looked around and realized that only Edge and Gideon Doyle had witnessed the one-sided quarrel, her unattractive and careworn face expressed shame.

"My troubles ain't nothin' compared with what's ailin' others tonight," she murmured as Edge struck a match on the cemetery wall and lit his freshly rolled cigarette.

"We all got our little problems, Mrs. Carlin, ma'am," Doyle allowed sympathetically.

The woman nodded, then sighed and said anxiously: "Maybe there's nothin' goin' on between my Nathan and her, but it sure does seem strange. . . ."

Her voice trailed away. Most of her fellow citizens were complying with Morrow's instructions to disperse, and she joined them.

"My problem right now, mister," the black man said, "is that you left me the makin's but I didn't have no match to light up with."

Edge had been about to drop the flickering match as he made an impassive survey of the frightened townspeople. Now he extended the match toward Doyle and growled: "Just like the lady said, feller."

The black man expressed puzzlement as he lit the cigarette.

Edge dropped the match and stepped on it. With a humorless grin added: "There's no smoke without fire."

Chapter Ten

GIDEON DOYLE removed the cigarette from his mouth long enough to direct a globule of saliva at the ground between his booted feet. Then said: ''That ain't a comment on your joke, mister. But I reckon a lot of other times I most probably would have laughed my balls off at it.''

''No sweat,'' the half-breed answered evenly. And, like the black man, did not move his cold eyes from the knot of Loganville citizens left on the center of the street. ''To most people's way of thinking there's a time and a place for everything.''

''Oh shit,'' Doyle groaned. ''I reckon this is the wrong time for me to be in this here place.''

It was the sight of Sheriff Rich Morrow striding toward him that drew this response. But it was not the sight of Doyle outside of the jailhouse that triggered the lawman's glowering anger. His temper had started to fray as he listened to the earnest and conspiritorial discussion among the group he had now swung away from. A group composed of Emily Bass, Sam Dyer, Glen Potts, Horace Quigley, Ansel Twist, and two women and four men whose names the half-breed did not know. He did know that everyone but the elderly owner of the hardware store had been supporters of the blacksmith's plan to give the killers the horses.

"Reckon I don't have to ask who let you out of my jailhouse?" Morrow said sourly. And glanced over his shoulder at the men and women who had triggered his anger as they moved off along Main Street.

Horace Quigley made haste to spread the word of their decision but the others were less eager. Some directed doleful glances toward the scowling lawman, but none came even close to asking him to reconsider his decision. Nor did anybody give any sign that he or she even saw the Negro and the half-breed.

"I was supposed to get turned loose anyway, Mr. Morrow," Doyle defended. "And I told Mr. Edge I wasn't gonna leave the jail until you give the all-clear. But what with all the shootin' and people runnin' and—"

"The hell with it, Doyle!" Morrow cut in sourly. "You and your fast-gun buddy are the least of my worries right now! I have to do something real fast before their next half-baked plan puts more lives at risk!"

The scowl lines cut deeper into his haggard face as he slammed a tight fist into an open palm and stared out of wearied eyes along the main street of what was no longer his town. And was obviously peering into a middle distance that was not peopled with his fellow citizens.

He was not aware of the man after whose family name the town had been called until Spiro Logan was just a few yards away, grinning broadly with relief as he reported: "Kent's going to be fine, Rich. He's bruised some and the shock'll take awhile to go away, Doc Corrigan says. Knocked himself out when he tripped and fell. He's awake now, dizzy but able to remember and talk. Seems that when the shooting started he just saw his chance and made a run and a jump through the broken window. There was no time to tell the other children and Miss Heller what he had in mind. Just time to up and do it. Guess he knew he was taking a chance. If there had been time . . . knowing my boy the way I do . . . well, he wouldn't have asked anyone else to take the risk with him. And he'd have figured out that if he made it, there'd be one less hostage for us to worry about."

"That's fine, Mr. Logan," the lawman said absently, his anger seemingly exhausted as he turned to peer at the school in the cottonwood grove.

"Boy, when I saw his hands as he went down . . . plain as day in the moonlight. All that red. I was sure it was blood. But it was just ink, though. The others are in the same state. Seems the four of them fooling around with the ink and getting it all over themselves was the reason the teacher held them back in school past time."

The rancher in the mud-spattered dudish garb was abruptly drained of his elation and only now became aware that the three other men standing beside the cemetery wall on the rapidly emptying street were paying scant attention to what he said.

"Oh, yeah," he went on lamely. "Doc Corrigan says that old man Kyne has got a better than even chance of making it."

"That's good, Mr. Logan," Doyle said with feeling. "Mr. Kyne is a fine man. And the only kin that his grandson's got left in the world, way I hear it."

"You heard it right, swillbelly," Morrow confirmed absently as he continued to peer toward the school.

Doyle spit between his boots again and then scowled at the broad back of the lawman as he rasped: "A couple of drinks to celebrate him findin' a good woman to take care of him and a no-account nigger's a swillbelly! The town drunk's white as snow so he ain't—"

"Shut up!" Morrow snarled. "Shut your stinking mouth while I'm trying to think!"

"Easy, Rich," Logan placated.

The sheriff whipped into a half turn from the waist, his eyes blazing and his teeth bared. For a stretched second he looked on the point of hurling a string of obscenities at the rancher. Then, as he began to clench and unclench his hands, there seemed a danger he was even going to launch himself at the suddenly grim-faced man.

"What half-baked plan, feller?" Edge asked evenly, and captured the wild-eyed attention of the lawman.

"What?" Morrow rapped out the monosyllable through his gritted teeth like it was a curse.

"Figure you and me are on the same line of thought."

"A gunslinger who reads minds yet?" Morrow sneered, contempt displacing rage on his gaunt face. He swept his gaze over each man in turn and challenged with a grim smile: "Well then, you'll be able to tell this no-account nigger—his words, not mine—and our local figure of power and influence just how *I* plan to bring the lawbreakers to book?"

Then he untwisted from the waist and strode off along the trail.

"Sonofabitch, that struttin' lawman's gone off his friggin' rocker at last," Gideon Doyle muttered in a tone of awe. "I always said he might and now—"

"Rich, don't do anything to—" Logan cut in. The words were suddenly trapped in his throat as he saw a movement on the periphery of his vision. He snapped his head around to stare at Edge, making a sound somewhere between a sigh and a gasp, as he saw that the impassive stranger had stayed his right hand, which had gripped the butt of the holstered Colt.

And now Logan returned his gaze to Morrow and along with Edge and Doyle watched the sheriff veer off the trail toward the moon-shadowed trees.

"Goddammit, I was sure he was going to just walk up to the school and call those two men out for a showdown," the rancher muttered in a tone of astonishment.

"You ain't the only one around here figured that, Mr. Logan," the black man added pointedly, and both of them looked at the half-breed, who now let go of his gun—and then emphasized his decision not to draw it by fastening the buttons of his coat.

"He didn't seem to be in any mood to pay attention to what anyone else wanted, Mr. Edge," Logan said, relief making his tone perhaps lighter than he intended.

"Wasn't going to argue with him," Edge said evenly as all three of them glanced indifferently at the elderly town gossip, who was moving dejectedly along the street toward them. "Was going to kill him."

"You better believe it," Gideon Doyle murmured.

Logan gazed hard at the impassive face with the slitted eyes glittering so coldly through the drifting cigarette smoke. And nodded knowingly as he said: "I do. I believe it."

"I reckon you folks all know how Sam figures to get the kids and the Heller girl away from the killers?" Horace Quigley asked, his tone a match for his despondent expression and disconsolate gait. "Nobody else in this town wants to know . . . almost like they figure that if they don't know nothin' about it, they can't have none of the blame for not tryin' to talk him out of it if it goes wrong. Suppose Rich told you men?"

"No, Mr. Quigley," Logan replied, interested.

"That lawman don't never talk to me unless it's to take a swipe at me on account of my color," Doyle added, and made to straighten up and swing away from the other men.

"Don't go too far, feller," Edge drawled, and as Doyle came to a halt with a grunt of surprise, continued to the brightening Quigley: "Your local sheriff figures me for a gunslinger and a mind reader. Nobody can be wrong about everything. So maybe he's third time right to think Dyer's idea stinks?"

"You know I make a charge, mister," Doyle reminded, smiling at the half-breed in anticipation of raising some money.

"You lost me, stranger," the elderly store keeper said, puzzled.

After shooting an anxious glance at the horses, which were being led from out of the livery and the alley between the stage-line depot and the corral, Spiro Logan rasped: "*I'm* telling you to keep your mouth shut now, Doyle! And your color's got nothing to do with it! What the stranger means, Mr. Quigley, is that he would very much like to hear about Sam Dyer's intentions!" He directed another sidelong look down the street and concluded: "Without any frills, please. Or we may be able to witness it before you are through telling us of it."

The tall and skinny old-timer kept nodding as the rancher was talking, patently anxious for him to be through so he could begin. Then: "Him and young Potts . . . that's Sam and Glen Potts . . . they're gonna exchange themselves for the little ones and the Heller girl, Mr. Logan. Emily Bass wanted to go with the killers in exchange for them they got in the schoolhouse. And a whole bunch of other folks was willin' to . . ."

Edge listened impassively, Gideon Doyle continued to show a faint smile of avaricious expectation, and Spiro Logan was having difficulty containing his impatience. Each time the rancher glared back at Quigley after glancing along the street, the old-timer was in danger of losing the thread of his story.

"But that ain't neither here nor there, is it? Sam said

he was gonna go for sure on account of it was his idea. And that young feller that works for you out at the Meadowlark Ranch, Mr. Logan . . . well, he said he wasn't gonna let them men that killed his kid brother outta his sight before he had a chance to . . . Later, of course. Oh, well, upshot was that Sam and him are gonna go.''

The clop of hooves as horses were walked slowly along Main Street drew the attention of all four men toward the intersection at the center of Loganville. They saw Dyer and Potts each leading two horses by the reins.

''See, just like I told you,'' Quigley exclaimed in the excited manner of somebody who considered his word had been doubted and was now vindicated.

''That it, feller?''

''Uh?'' the old-timer grunted as a group of his fellow citizens gathered on the intersection behind the men with the horses. They formed a less closely knit assemblage than had supported the blacksmith earlier and were far fewer in number, no more than a score of men and women. And they did not fall in behind the four horses but remained scattered across the intersection, waiting and watching.

''Just going to tell the two fellers in the schoolhouse what they have in mind and trust in whatever they believe that Benedict Ives and Animal—''

''Yeah, Stranger,'' Quigley answered quizzically. ''Far as I know, and Sam Dyer was all through tellin' it before I left. Them killers said they was just gonna take the two people when they pulled out, didn't they? Why should they care if it's two outta the four they already got or two different ones?'' He shrugged his narrow shoulders.

Edge looked questioningly at Doyle, in much the same way that Logan was eyeing him, while Horace Quigley devoted his full attention to Dyer and Potts.

''It's my guess Animal will go along with whatever Ives says, mister,'' Gideon Doyle growled uncertainly, his head bowed while he mashed his discarded cigarette butt into the mud—and kept mashing after it was out. ''And that Ives guy . . . well, he's likely to do just about anythin'. Go for it, or just start blastin' away on account of people ain't done exactly like he told them. I just don't know about him, Mr. Edge, sir.''

''You know those men in the school, Doyle?'' Logan demanded incredulously.

''Not so that it amounts to much, Mr. Logan, sir,'' the black man answered, as Horace Quigley became as avidly interested in what he had to say as was the rancher.

But then the scowling Dyer and the grim-faced Potts ordered the horses to a halt a few yards away. And while the young ranch hand gazed fixedly toward Abner Coburn, who was still crouched at the schoolyard wall, the powerfully built blacksmith warned: ''Have to presume you men been told by Quigley what me and young Potts here are about. Now give you fair warnin', same as I did to Rich Morrow . . . and hope he's told the men he deputized the same. Any attempt to take a hand in this unless me and this young man have been shot dead . . .'' He drew in a deep breath and gestured with a movement of his head back along the street. "Well, if Potts nor me are in any shape to make you pay the price for interferin' in what's none of your concern, others will be."

The people on the intersection did not move. And perhaps their utter stillness was more meancing than if they had voiced their will to vengeance and displayed an arsenal of weaponry.

"Mr. Dyer, Potts!" Spiro Logan said urgently. "Doyle here knows the men in the school!" He shot a nervous glance at the half-breed, his eyes pleading. "And I think Edge has a plan that might be more likely to succeed than—"

"Your youngster is free of those killers, Mr. Logan," the blacksmith cut in resolutely, his scowl replaced by icy determination. "Old Ira Kyne ain't in any condition to help get his grandson away from them. And little Lauren Bass don't have no Pa to go fight for her no more. But I'm still here and in one piece, and while my Emily and them other kids are still in the clutches of them murderin' sonsofbitches, I ain't gonna stay back and—"

"You assholes out there!" Benedict Ives bellowed from the schoolhouse, which was hidden from the six men on the end of Main Street. "How long does it take a bunch of hicks to saddle up four friggin' horses? You don't hurry it up, I'll show you how long it takes to rid the world of a couple of snivelin' brats!"

"You got the right, feller," Edge told Sam Dyer, who for part of a second after Ives completed the threat looked to be losing his nerve. "All I got is an idea."

146

Neither Glen Potts nor Sam Dyer gave any indication that he had heard what the half-breed said as they started forward with the horses.

"Mr. Logan, sir?" Doyle said morosely.

"Doyle?"

"I'm fixin' to marry Betsy Blake pretty soon."

While all other eyes stayed fixed on Dyer and Potts as they closed with the cottonwood grove, Spiro Logan found himself looking in amazement at the Negro. Then he shrugged and in the manner of somebody humoring another, answered: "I'm pleased for you. And Betsy Blake."

"Be lookin' for steadier-type work than what I been doin', sir. Odd jobbin' and the like."

"Good grief, Doyle, this is hardly the time and—" Quigley began. The loudness of his voice struck a sour note in the taut silence, which had been strangely unaffected by the low toned exchange between Doyle and Logan. An admonishing glower from the rancher caused the old-timer to abandon his rebuke with a grimace of indignation and then to growl resentfully.

"Figure the feller is getting around to making a point?" Edge suggested with an impassive glance at Doyle as he dropped his cigarette butt and unfastened the buttons of his sheepskin coat again.

The glance invited the Negro to say what was on his mind and the unbuttoning of the coat allowed for easier access to the holstered Colt in the event of expected trouble. This as the men with the horses—in clear sight of the two in the school now—came close enough to Coburn, still crouched at the wall, for Dyer and the liveryman to exchange an inaudible whisper.

"You already lost one of your hands tonight, Mr. Logan. And if Ives and Animal go for the switch of hostages, I'm tellin' you that you're gonna lose the services of the other Potts brother, sir. I ain't one to make hay outta other folks' troubles, but facts is facts and the fact is the Meadowlark spread is already one man short and will likely be short another before—"

"I'll keep you in mind, Doyle."

"I ain't got no skills with cows, of course—"

"If you're all so sure that they're goin' to get killed, we ought to—" Quigley cut in anxiously, becoming increasingly agitated at the way the trio of men with him sought to bury their own disquiet with apparently detached talk.

"They're in no mood to listen, let alone to take advice," Logan growled as he continued to gaze fixedly at Dyer and Potts, who were aligning the four horses on the threshold of the schoolyard. "I guess you could learn, Doyle?"

"Sure is right, on both counts, sir," the Negro answered.

"Town will be short a man too, feller," the half-breed reminded as the old-timer had to make a considerable effort to keep from snarling with fury. "And you look to be better suited to fill the empty place there'll be for a blacksmith."

"Is that supposed to be some kind of joke, stranger?" Horace Quigley asked, his voice husky with suppressed anger as he wrenched his head from side to side, desperately searching for some sign of fellow feeling from somebody.

148

And then a guffaw of laughter brought the lengthy silence in the schoolhouse to an abrupt end.

Edge rasped through tightly gritted teeth: "Seems somebody has a taste for black humor."

Chapter Eleven

IT WAS the short and flabby, scar-faced Animal who had erupted into nervous laughter at the sight of Dyer and Potts taking so much trouble to arrange themselves and the horses in the gap in the wall. But the laughter died in his throat when the taller, leaner, younger but more mature Benedict Ives snarled: "Quit it, asshole! Unless you wanna maybe die laughin'!"

These were the first words that had been spoken within the faintly moonlit classroom for what seemed to the hostages an inordinately long time.

But it had only been a few minutes since Ives saw the last of the townspeople move off the trail beyond the trees, which obscured all of Loganville except the church and a section of the cemetery wall. He and Animal had donned their still-wet hats and long coats, Animal transferring the stolen money from Pierce Starky's coat to his own.

Arlene Heller, clasping the two small girls to her while Marvin James insisted upon remaining a little apart from the group, looked on with hope in her red-rimmed eyes and dread in her anguished mind as she watched these preparations for departure. Sometimes Emily Dyer or Lauren Bass whimpered their fear and occasionally the boy muttered one of the many obscenities he had picked up from his grandfather. Arlene murmured to the girls that everything would be all right soon, directed a rebuking look at Marvin, who she guessed was torn between admiration for Kent Logan's opportune escape and contempt for what might have been the reckless act of a coward.

Then Animal started to complain that he could not see a thing in the shadowed timber behind the school-house. And Ives had allowed that the posse could easily reach the windows on that side of the classroom and not be spotted until they blasted bullets inside.

And there had been an eruption of fearful and tearful talk then, as Ives began to rasp orders to Animal and the hostages. Which immediately ceased when the taller man thrust the muzzle of a gun into the gaping mouth of the cursing Marvin James. As Marvin gagged on the evil-tasting gun barrel in his mouth, his torturer displayed a buck-toothed grin and quickly and quietly talked the woman and two small girls into horrified silence, saying how he would not hesitated to blast the boy's head off his shoulders. The tacit plea in Arlene Heller's wide eyes, however, seemed to mollify him.

Now they all stood in silence again, in the positions they had held since Ives yelled his threat to the children if the horses he had demanded were not brought soon.

He was at the door, one of his green eyes close to the inch-wide gap, the muzzle of one of his Colts aimed over the sprawled corpse of Pierce Starky at Sam Dyer.

Animal stood at the side of the glassless window, a gun fisted in each of his fleshy hands. Arlene Heller was forced to stand in front of him, held tight by his left arm across her belly. His right arm pressed a revolver muzzle into her pulsing and sweaty neck.

The Colt in his left hand was aimed at the three children, who stood in a huddle on top of their teacher's desk, so that the danger they were in would be obvious to anyone who got close enough to peer in.

On the pleading instructions of Arlene Heller, the young James boy had ceased cursing and assumed her role of comforting the small girls. The three children melded into a tableau of pitiable vulnerability on the desk top. Arlene's concern for the children forced her to maintain her self-control. She knew that had all of them gotten away with Kent Logan, she would by now have lost her reason.

For the man she loved was dead. When she peered out through the window where Animal pushed her and saw Glen Potts with Sam Dyer, she finally had to accept what she had suspected. Rod was dead and she was the captive of two crazed killers, one of whom she could feel moving against her lustfully as he obeyed the other's command to be silent. His erection between her thighs was almost as horrifying to her as the gun muzzle in her neck. And she was sure she was on the brink of unconsciousness—perhaps even madness—that she was only able to hold back from because of the children.

"All right, you assholes!" Ives shouted through the

door. "Bring the mounts over here to where Starky's stretched out! And if any of you guys with the guns want to try your luck, you friggin' go right ahead! You can see the spot the little lady teacher is in, I figure?"

There was no response as Dyer and Potts led the horses slowly into the schoolyard.

"Answer me, frig it!" Ives thundered.

He shot a glaring glance at Animal, who vented another nervous laugh and took a step foward, this movement of his aroused body forcing Arlene Heller into greater prominence at the window. It also meant that he was more plainly seen, but he was shielded by the terrified woman.

"Everyone can see her!" Glen Potts blurted.

And it seemed as if the blacksmith had been dumbstruck until now. For he shook his head vigorously, as if to clear it of whatever was paralysing his mental functions, and announced vehemently: "We told Sheriff Morrow to tell the men he deputized not to open fire unless you start in to kill the hostages, Ives!"

"Well, they better do like you told them, asshole. On account of—"

"Time for threats is gone!" Dyer cut in as he and Potts halted near the dead man sprawled on the drying mud of the yard. "Gonna tell you and your partner what's gonna happen now! Me and young Potts here are gonna mount up on two of these horses and we're gonna ride out of Loganville with you! And the children and Miss Heller are gonna be set free and—"

Benedict Ives gave vent to an animalistic roar of demented rage that seemed beyond the range of the human vocal chords. And, in fact, his voice broke and the shriek became a gasp at the same moment as he flung open the door. Dyer and Potts instinctively hurled themselves to the ground in expectation of a hail of bullets, dropping to their knees and throwing themselves sideways. Groans of despair wailed from their throats as they saw they had mistaken what Ives intended to do and were now helpless to prevent him.

For the crashing open of the door had revealed the huddle of frail forms atop the desk. And they could see too the gun in the fist of the otherwise unseen man as he aimed at the frozen-with-terror children.

But Arlene Heller was not powerless. For the man who moments before had held her in an imprisoning and sexual embrace had been as disconcerted as anybody else at his partner's mindless rage, had seemed to forget about her entirely as he wrenched his gaze from the shrieking Ives to stare out of the window in search of whatever had unbalanced the man.

And now, perhaps plunging off the brink into a madness of her own, the tall and slender schoolteacher tore free of her captor, channeling every ounce of frenzied strength into a lunge at the man who was about to gun down the howling and cursing children. She vented her own furious scream as she threw herself at Ives, compelling the man to snap his head around and peer at her. Just for a moment ice-cold terror replaced his rage as she clawed at him, an expression of vicious hatred on her face. But then his instinct for self-preservation asserted itself. He had taken his finger off the trigger of the Colt. Because he had been able to control the urge to panic, he did not tighten his finger again until he had swung the revolver around to draw a bead on the mask of malevolence that so contorted the woman's face.

His bullet drove into one of her blazing eyes and the force of its impact jerked her head back and around as her brain died but her forward momentum was not halted.

Emily and Lauren screamed more shrilly and Marvin's voice was suddenly hoarse with the effort of shouting. All three children were rooted to the desk as they watched the now silent and almost serene Benedict Ives. Saw the man step smoothly out of the path of the forward-moving corpse with its blood-gushing eye socket, then charge into it with a shoulder and hip as it began to fall. So that the suddenly limp and lifeless form of what had once been their teacher went hurtling over the threshold and across the porch to crash in the yard, close to the corpse of Pierce Starky.

A few feet away, Sam Dyer and Glen Potts held their breath, their eyes and mouths wide. Just for a moment they could have been mistaken for dead as the black-smith stared fixedly through the doorway and past Ives at the children, and the ranch hand's attention was transfixed by Animal who aimed both his guns out through the window at him and Dyer.

Then, as the horses that had backed off from the sounds and sights and smells of gun violence whinnied and began to prance skittishly around the confined space of the schoolyard, Dyer gasped: "Oh, my God . . . Arlene."

Potts pleaded to Animal: "Whatever you want, mister?"

The flabby, short, scar-faced man at the window had

seen enough out in the night to know there was no immediate danger and was able to think clearly enough to realize mere words had driven Benedict Ives to homicidal craziness. He stepped back from the window as the children on the desk top drew closer together, sobbing. Said loudly enough for his voice to carry outside: "Three kids are all we got left, Ives!"

"I can friggin' count, asshole!" the taller, younger man snarled. Then he kicked the door violently closed. And ignored the trembling, quietening hostages and the perplexed Animal as he bellowed at the door: "You brought the horses, hicks! Just like I told you! But I didn't say for you to tell me what to do! So the teacher got herself killed from bein' stupid after you was stupid! You hear me good, assholes?"

"This is Sheriff Morrow and I—" the lawman, who was crouched with the big Walker Colt drawn, called from the other side of the gateway to Coburn.

"Frig it, I ain't talkin' to you!" Ives roared. "I'm talkin' to the hick that figured he could tell me what to do and got the teacher lady killed for his mistake!"

"I hear you, mister," Sam Dyer answered wretchedly.

"So listen to me good, asshole," the tall, lean man rasped less loudly as he pushed his angular face close to the door panel. "You and that other hick you got with you round up them four horses from all over the friggin' yard and hitch them to the porch posts. Then get the hell away from here. And tell that tough-talkin' lawman of yours to get the hell away to boot. And he better move his deputies outta the trees and away from here. Gonna give you assholes fifteen minutes to fix all that up for me. And then me and Animal are gonna leave this stinkin' schoolhouse in this stinkin' town. Gonna leave or gonna die here. But we won't die at the ends of no lynch ropes, assholes. You and the other hicks'll have to shoot us down. Can't say how many more of you hicks we'll take with us. Above three, that is. Although they're such itsy-bitsy little hick assholes maybe it can't be figured that all three of them amount to one full grown, truth to tell?''

His protruding teeth were revealed beneath his bushy mustache in a grin that seemed almost genial in the dim moonlit classroom as he turned to look at the still and silent children. Then he showed something akin to puzzlement as he faced the door again before a silent snarl spread across his features as he warned: ''I don't hear any friggin' movement out there and I already told you there ain't no more than fifteen minutes to get done what you gotta do!''

His smile now was certainly one of genuine pleasure as he swung completely around and leaned his back against the wall. Listened to the footfalls of men and the clop of hooves on the surface of the schoolyard for several moments, then said evenly to the exhausted children: ''See, gang? Your uncle Benedict figures you been too long at school already and is makin' real sure you get out real soon now.''

''You're not our uncle,'' the nine-year-old Emily Dyer countered, biting her lip as she struggled against more tears.

''And we hate you, both of you!'' the year-older Lauren Bass said in a stronger voice with a toss of her head that set her red hair swinging.

''You're sonsofbitches that stink higher than my

grandpa's hogs is what you are, you bastards!'' the twelve-year-old Marvin James accused, looking more like his grandfather than ever.

''You got a bad mouth I'm gonna enjoy shuttin', kid!'' Animal rasped.

Ives chuckled and he taunted the man at the window: ''Kids is all they all are, pal. And you didn't oughta allow them to get to you that way.'' Then, as he shifted his green eyes away from Animal to the trio of children, his smile became a salacious leer. And he growled as his gaze lingered on the slender forms of the two girls: ''In other ways, maybe, though.''

Animal spat at the floor, and this drew a scowl from Ives. But Sam Dyer spoke before Ives could counter the implied insult.

''Horses are hitched like you wanted, mister.''

Animal glanced out the window and nodded to his partner that Dyer was speaking the truth.

''So time's a-wastin', asshole,'' Ives answered. ''Get the hell away like you was told.''

''Like to move Arlene's body to the undertaking parlor?'' Glen Potts posed tentatively.

''You take the teacher, you take old Pierce along with her and—''

''Leave them both where they are, assholes!'' Benedict Ives interrupted Animal, his voice again enraged. He had to make a conscious effort, visible to Animal, to add menacingly: ''Remind all you hicks just how dead assholes that cross me can get. Now beat it.''

Animal looked outside again and saw Dyer and Potts backing away slowly from the quartet of horses hitched to the archway. Then the two men turned and broke into a

159

run toward the gateway, where Morrow and Coburn rose into sight at each side. The liveryman had a repeater rifle and the sheriff was still holding his big handgun. But as they listened to the blacksmith, neither man aimed his weapon at the schoolhouse each time his concerned attention was drawn there.

"They're doin' what you told them, Ives," Animal reported.

"Like I can count, I can hear good too," Ives responded sourly, then clicked his fingers and grinned. "Hey, count. You kids can do that, I figure?"

"Of course we can," Emily Dyer replied indignantly. And grimaced as Lauren Bass dug an elbow in her ribs and Marvin James made a sound of disgust.

"So that's what you're all gonna do," Ives instructed evenly. "To sixty. Twelve times, one to sixty, because I figure the grown-ups outside have already used three of the fifteen minutes I give them."

"Go to hell, you—" the boy snarled.

"You got a lot of guts, kid," Ives cut in on him, but it was his Colt rather than his voice that caused the youngster to bite back the words. "No brains, though. So I reckon I'll plug you in the belly and watch your guts run out so you'll match up real well."

"You need us so you won't!"

"I count three of you and just one'll be enough, kid. One . . . two . . . three . . . four . . ." Ives tracked the revolver from one to the other as he began the slow count, then halted at the boy.

"Five, six, seven—he'll do it, Marv, I know he will—eight, nine, ten," Lauren Bass blurted, with an imploring look at the boy and the other girl.

Emily joined in the counting and then, after Ives had deliberately eased back the hammer of his Colt, the scowling boy made it a chorus of three. With the hammer still thumbed back, the grinning Ives used the revolver as a baton for a few moments, histrionically conducting the chanting voices of the defiantly reluctant trio.

The voices of the children, becoming more rhythmical with passing time and given a kind of sweetness of tone by distance, reached a considerable way into Loganville.

Edge, Gideon Doyle, and Spiro Logan heard them counting as they headed toward the crowd of watchers and waiters. Most of Loganville's citizens had emerged from their bolt holes to discover what new tragedy had been unleashed upon their community.

Many pairs of eyes peered quizzically at the three men for a moment or two and upon evoking no encouraging response most looked back along Main Street toward the two small groups of men at the far end. One group remained at the point where the street became the trail to Dodge City. The other, which included Horace Quigley, Sheriff Morrow, and Glen Potts, advanced on the intersection.

The dowdy and dumpy, wan and anxious Emily Bass asked of anyone who cared to answer: "The children?"

"All three of them is still fine, ma'am," Gideon Doyle replied as he turned onto River Road with Spiro Logan.

The rancher spotted somebody he was looking for in the crowd and said: "We could use your help with something that needs to be done out at old Ira Kyne's place, Mr. Eden?"

"Go with them, Ralph," the wife of the town butcher encouraged her reticent husband.

"What about Arl—Miss Heller—the schoolteacher, mister?" the gangling, morose-faced Ansel Twist asked as the half-breed headed through the mass of nervous people toward the batwing entrance of the Cottonwood saloon.

Edge looked impassively into the pale face of the youngster, who had already guessed the answer his query would bring, and growled: "Listen, feller."

Twist did listen to the far-off voices of the three children, who had begun counting the third minute. And gulped before he was able to force out: "I thought after Rod Potts got killed that I might stand a chance . . . she's gone, uh?"

"Like I said," Edge replied as he pushed open the swing doors. He saw that Patsy Blair was the only patron and added in a sardonic rasp so that only the full-bodied woman with the too yellow hair heard him: "Listen . . . it's just the kids who count now."

Chapter Twelve

THE CHANTING voices of the children, starting to sound ragged and husky, reached another "sixty" and then paused. Tension mounted until Benedict Ives cracked open the door of the schoolhouse and cupped his hands to his mouth as he yelled: "One minute to go, you assholes! Then me and my partner are leavin' this hick town! Long as you stay back like you been told, won't nothin' bad happen. . . ."

"Ives!" Animal snapped from beside the window as his partner's voice faded away.

Four men and a woman had appeared beyond the corner of the schoolyard to surprise Ives into nervous silence and force the anxious single syllable from Animal.

"I got friggin' eyes!" the top man of the partnership snarled, then raised his voice again, but dropped his hands to his holstered Colts. "You assholes gotta have

163

the carcass of one of these brats before you take my word I mean what I friggin' say?''

Edge was at the head of the line of five as they emerged from behind the screen of cottonwoods that hid the schoolhouse from the town. As he scanned the front of the building he saw a movement at the shattered window. But just the voice of Benedict Ives pinpointed his position at the door within the shadowed porch.

The horses hitched at the porch, two at either side, were quiet. Close by them on the crusted mud surface of the softly moonlit yard were the corpses of Pierce Starky and Arlene Heller. In the chill night air after the rainstorm, the strongest smell in the area of the Loganville schoolhouse was of fear.

The half-breed's disquiet had first stirred as he left the saloon with the Widow Blair, Sheriff Morrow, Spiro Logan, and Gideon Doyle, the five of them moving as a loose-knit cluster then, past the people on the midtown intersection. Not a word spoken. But a hundred and one feelings expressed on the faces of the watchers, running the gamut from despair to hope. Here and there a flicker of animosity. The five who moved at the unhurried pace along the deserted western stretch of Main Street maintained an impassive mask to conceal their own emotions. All made whatever effort was required to achieve this until they had passed beyond the funeral parlor, where all three members of the Rankinn family were attending to the dead, and the building in which Doc Corrigan was tending young Kent Logan and old Ira Kyne.

It was then, as, by prearrangement, they fell into the ordered line, that they felt able to abandon their stoical facades. For in such a formation even those in a position to see one another had only a rear view. But most, as they allowed their trepidation to show in a frown or grimace, were aware of the others feeling much as they did.

Edge was the most experienced at coping with fear and knew how to harness it as an aid to concentration and sharpener of reflexes. He was less used to self-doubt, which was what had been threatening to throw his thinking into a turmoil ever since he stepped through the batwings of the Cottonwood and surveyed the sea of faces before him. Doubt about the wisdom of what he was doing—what he was responsible for the others doing, also—was likely to have the opposite effect of the plain and simple, far more familiar, fear of getting killed.

When the children ended their count and the raucous voice of Benedict Ives yelled its threat, the half-breed came close to aborting his plan. And he knew with total certainty at that moment that the people in the line behind him would have responded instantly and with unbounded relief to the decision.

Patsy Blair was immediately in back of him and he had heard her striving to control her breathing as they came closer to their objective and the effect of the final shot of rye rapidly wore off. Behind her was Rich Morrow, who had been the hardest to convince. But as the counting chant of the children in the distance emphasized the shortening time—while Edge worked on the bullets and Logan and Doyle and Ralph Eden returned from the hog and chicken farm—the lawman finally agreed to the half-breed's plan. As he helped the Negro empty and refill the bottles, he talked persuasively to

Emily Bass and Sam Dyer to keep them from wavering. He would be concerned about the safety of the children, Edge was sure of that. And maybe too he'd be anxiously aware of the possibility he could get himself killed and harboring a worry about how the people of Loganville viewed his handling of the siege at the school. Perhaps he hoped that a successful outcome to this play would put a new sheen on his tarnished image.

Come to hink of it, this was Patsy Blair's primary, perhaps only, reason for agreeing so readily to the half-breed's request. A display of heroism would do her sullied reputation no harm.

The rancher who was next in the line? Edge had a suspicion that Spiro Logan was troubled on at least two counts. That people might consider his son a coward for breaking out of the schoolhouse and leaving the others still captive. And he was nursing a nagging resentment that it was Edge and not himself who had made the dash through a hail of crossfire to snatch up the unconscious boy. But soon fear of death would negate such considerations. Just as Gideon Doyle on the end of the line would be unable to exclude the dread of dying from his hope for regular and better paid work as a result of aiding Loganville in its hour of desperate need.

Now, in the tense silence after Benedict Ives's menacing question, the half-breed ceased speculating about his fellow conspirators' thoughts. His lean, dark-skinned, heavily bristled face was set in its usual impassive lines; not an iota of debilitating doubt was allowed to dull his readiness to prove himself a more efficient killer than the men in the schoolhouse.

"Got a proposition to put to you, feller," Edge said,

not shouting, as he halted on the far side of the gateway and turned to face the schoolhouse yard.

"I already made one, and it's the only one there is, asshole!" Ives snarled as the others in the line closed rank and turned to face him. Ives and Animal could see that the coatless half-breed and lawman each had a gun in his holster, while the woman, the rancher, and the Negro all wore coats but no hats against the chill of the night.

Neither of the apprehensively intrigued men in the schoolhouse were in a frame of mind to note that Logan wore Edge's sheepskin coat. And neither were they disposed to consider the fact that the entire adult population of Loganville might be silently watching along Main Street—and were so seen by Doyle and Morrow, who had not been able to resist a glance to their right as they made the turn at the gateway.

"Tell him, Doyle," Edge said, loud enough for the men in the schoolhouse to hear.

"Animal!" the Negro called, and groaned in embarrassment at how nervous he sounded. Managed to pitch his voice at a more natural tone: "Hey, man, this is Gideon Doyle, the no-account nigger. You remember me, Animal?"

"I'll be a sonofabitch!" the man at the side of the window countered. He leaned fully into view, but then drew sharply back when Ives rasped a warning to him. He was just as jubilant, though, when he confirmed: "Course I recall you, pal! In the Omaha pokey where I busted out and you didn't on account of your time was almost—"

167

"What the frig is this?" Ives roared. "A friggin' reunion, you assholes?"

Then he muttered something to his partner that was incomprehensible to those out on the trail. And a subservient Animal growled: "You know about me, pal. Ives is worse, I reckon. You tell them people with you we ain't gonna do no dickerin' or nothin'."

"I told them about you already, Animal. And I told them what I heard about Benedict Ives."

"If it was nothin' good, then it was likely the truth," Ives put in.

Doyle was momentarily disconcerted by the interruption and Morrow made a clucking noise of impatience that acted to urge the Negro to continue.

"That's just it, mister. If what you didn't already do hereabouts didn't make Loganville folks know you'd kill them little ones easy as winkin', then what I told them sure made them see the light."

"So what's all this proposition crap the hick at the head of the line handed out?" Ives demanded.

"You're just too damn mean, feller," Edge told him. "You can't be trusted to be let out of town with the kids. The townspeople would rather have them killed clean with bullets here and see you pay the price . . . than to risk you getting away with it after—"

"We wouldn't—" Animal cut in.

"Shut up!" Ives snarled, and during the silence that ensued, everyone in the gateway held their breath in fear that Ives would blast the children. Only the pitiful whimpering of one of the small girls kept the silence from being absolute. Then, sounding coldly self-composed, Ives said: "Time for threatenin' is all over and done, asshole?'' Just a slight change in his tone turned what could have been an ultimatun into a query.

Edge said: "We make an exchange of hostages, Ives. Feller standing next to Doyle is Spiro Logan. The town's named after his family and he's the biggest rancher in the county. Very important man. Lady next to me is the Widow Blair. She's the sheriff's lady. That's the sheriff between her and Logan." As he spoke of the past Edge realized that another reason for the woman being here was to hear her name linked once more with that of Rich Morrow. "Both of them are volunteers, Ives," the half-breed went on. "They know what kind of risks they'll be running, leaving town as your prisoners. And you'll know nobody from Loganville will take a chance on trying to get you until—''

"I got the drift, hick," Ives cut in. "How do I know she's the woman of the asshole with the tin star and the one with the white hair's the local big shot?"

"Doyle?" Animal posed.

"This is Mr. Spiro Logan sure enough and Patsy Blair is—''

"He's a nigger in a white town!" Ives snarled.

"He was in the jailhouse before I sprung him after hearing what he had to say about you fellers," Edge corrected. "And if it matters, I'm a passing-through stranger with no ax to grind.''

There was another tense pause, the silence now total. Then Animal made a rasping comment and Ives told him to shut up while he was thinking. The silence lasted several moments longer before Ives demanded sullenly: "Reckon a smart-assed hard nose like you got somethin' worked out how the switch can be made?''

Morrow caught his breath, Patsy Blair sighed, and Logan gulped. Gideon Doyle said, just audibly: "Sonofabitch."

Edge answered: "Simple's best, feller. Logan and the lady'll move out to the center of the schoolyard and wait there until the kids get level with them. Then the kids'll keep on coming toward us here and Logan and the lady'll head on to the schoolhouse. It all works out right, the sheriff and Doyle and me'll take the kids into town and you can ride on out soon as you're ready."

"We're ready, are we friggin' ready!" Animal growled with feeling.

"I'm thinkin, goddammit!" Ives told him.

"Once you've released Mr. Logan and the Widow Blair, I'll be telegraphing every law office in the state and—" Morrow began assertively.

"Shut your goddamn mouth, lawman!" Ives snarled. And in the same tone continued: "All right, you got yourself a deal, asshole! You brats, get down off that desk and over here to the door! Logan and the dame, start walkin' toward me!"

"Oh, my God!" Patsy Blair gasped.

"He went for it too damn easy!" Morrow murmured tautly.

"He's a crazy man we have to take a chance with," Edge said evenly.

Logan nodded his head decisively and said as he took a first step through the gateway: "That's right, it's now or never."

The full-bodied woman with the dyed blond hair moved off alongside the taller, older man. Both of them tentatively raised their arms to shoulder level, crooked up at the elbows as the children were heard to leap off the desk to the boarded floor.

The three men left in the gateway made no move to close up the gaps on either side of Rich Morrow. Gideon Doyle began to mutter but ceased abruptly as the door opened at the rear of the shadowed porch. Then, against the murky moonlight that entered the classroom and revealed that the door was open, the three small children were seen as a single, huddled-together silhouette.

Ives said something to them, soft but harsh. And they remained standing there in silence. One of them—the boy—was seen to be a head taller than the taller of the two girls.

Edge scowled while his hooded eyes continued to glitter icily as he chided himself for taking note of such inconsequentials. Then his eyes darted back and forth in search of Animal at the window and Ives in the doorway. The men or their guns.

Logan was heard to whisper a single word to Patsy Blair and the two of them came to a halt in unison. The rancher's voice revealed no sign of jangling nerves when he instructed: "You will set the children free now. Marvin, Lauren, Emily . . . you'll walk, not run, to where Sheriff Morrow and Mr. Doyle and Mr. Edge are waiting."

"Okay, sir," the boy responded, his voice husky with suppressed excitement or the strain of controlling his fear.

"Hold it," Ives snapped. "What if Animal and me blast you two to kingdom come and keep the brats here, what then, asshole of a big-shot rancher?"

Patsy Blair was not quite able to stifle a sob and her

whole body shuddered. Then Spiro Logan replied, as even-toned as before: "You've been told what the people of Loganville feel about allowing you to leave this town with—"

"Yeah, yeah, all right!" Ives cut in resentfully. "But it's me gives the order for the brats to take off. So go on, you snivelin' little hicks. Take off. But remember what the big-shot rancher told you. No hightailin' it. Walk, nice and easy. All the way. Then you can be almost sure your uncle Benedict won't make it so you visit with your uncle Pierce and your skinny teacher." He laughed mirthlessly, then ordered: "Beat it!"

The three-headed silhouette moved through the gloomy light; even as the children stepped warily out of the porch they continued to appear to the tense watchers at the gateway as a single indistinct entity. But a few steps more and they had the space to spread themselves in the yard where they had so often played. They did not move far apart, though, but held each other's ink-stained hands—Marvin and Emily flanking Lauren.

The strain of their ordeal was plain on their faces, which were ashen in the moonlight, with eyes and lips and hair that looked to be solid black by contrast. As they gingerly shuffled around the corpses, fear emanated from them. But an underlying conflict of emotions simmered just beneath the brittle surface of their fearfulness. And it was alarmingly apparent that each of them might panic at any moment—and give way to either euphoria or hysteria as they dashed through a barrage of blazing gunfire for safety or oblivion.

"Easy, kids," Logan urged, and now there was a

tremor of strain in his voice as his bright eyes constantly flicked from the children to the schoolhouse.

Patsy Blair could not trust herself to speak. But she was able to smile encouragingly.

"Kent really okay, sir?" Marvin asked.

The rancher nodded.

"Really appreciate what you and Mrs. Blair are doin' for us," Lauren added.

The only response to this was a choked sob from Patsy Blair as the line of children moved past the two adults. Then the man started forward and she followed a second later.

"Get your asses over here," Ives rasped, the tension of his voice in clear contrast to the pure pleasure of Animal's voice as he murmured excitedly: "Sonofabitch, they're doin' it."

"They friggin' better!"

"All the way inside, Ives? I've had my fill of this place!"

Ever since the children had been ordered to leave the schoolhouse, Benedict Ives had shown his gunhand and half his face at a side of the doorway. Now, as Patsy Blair and Logan, arms aloft, advanced to a point midway between the entrance of the building and the gateway, he stepped fully onto the threshold and hissed through teeth clenched in a forced grin: "You and me both, pal. School's where folks go to get smart. And we're already that, huh? Same as the hot-shot rancher here and the little lady—if they don't do nothin' to show they're stupid. Hold it, right there!"

He had a gun in each hand, leveled from the hips. They remained in a rock-steady aim at Logan and Patsy

173

Blair while his glinting green eyes kept shifting between the new and the former hostages.

The new hostages came to a halt a foot or so short of the two corpses.

"You coverin' the brats, Animal?"

"Sure thing, Ives."

The grimly smiling man with the buck teeth beneath his bushy mustache could tell that the rancher and the widow were rigid with fear. And this knowledge bolstered his flagging confidence as he saw the children reach the gateway, so that neither his expression nor his tone of voice had much hint of effort as he said: "All right, pal: let's you and me get the hell away from this hick town."

At the gateway of the schoolyard, Edge ignored the children to concentrate upon what was taking place in the area of the building entrance. Gideon Doyle peered fixedly at the youngsters, tensed to lunge toward them at the first sign of a double-cross by the men in the schoolhouse or to cajole them into remaining calm if they seemed about to make a dash for safety before the trap could be sprung.

Between the Negro and the half-breed, Rich Morrow divided his attention between the children and the schoolhouse as he clenched and unclenched one hand, the one hanging close to the butt of the big Walker Colt in his holster. And it was the lawman who spoke before Doyle was ready—probably intent upon steadying his own nerve and calming the pale-faced, rigid, raggedly breathing children.

"You're doing fine," he murmured. "Just keep on coming like that. When you get closer, all of you move to the side and follow Doyle . . . Mr. Doyle. You all know him, don't you? Just come out through the gateway alongside me and go with Mr. Doyle. And do exactly what he tells you to do, okay?''

The glittering light in Edge's eyes got colder and he drew back his lips in a grimace. He wanted to tell the sheriff to shut up so he would be better able to hear what was being said at the schoolhouse. But he was afraid of tipping the fine balance of the children's emotional stability.

Then Doyle was stepping back and turning, gesturing for the youngsters to come out of the schoolyard and move along the trail toward town. And they did as they were instructed, letting go of each other's ink-stained hands to move in single file through the gateway: Emily Dyer, Lauren Bass, and Marvin James.

When all three were on the trail and starting for town ahead of the black man—needed, if necessary just to pitch to the ground behind the stone wall, safe from the guns of the killers—a mass sigh of relief reached out from the center of Loganville like the sound of a gentle summer breeze rustling the tops of tall trees.

If the two men in the schoolyard gateway heard this, or the soft-spoken words of Gideon Doyle as he coaxed the children to remain calm while they searched the crowd advancing along Main Street for a mother, two fathers, and a grandfather, they did not allow themselves to be distracted from their watch at the schoolhouse entrance. Where, partially obscured by the tall form of Spiro Logan and the shorter but broader frame of Patsy Blair, first Benedict Ives and then Animal stepped from out of the porch.

175

While Ives continued to aim both his Colts at the man and the woman, Animal slid his back in the holsters so he could unhitch the horses.

"Deal was for all you assholes to take off with the brats!" Ives commanded.

It could not have been predicted precisely what the top man in the partnership would say at this point. But this served as well as anything else.

Edge and Morrow began to swing toward the right and Logan and Patsy Blair turned to look over their shoulders. These moves natural enough. As was the manner in which Gideon Doyle shot a backward glance at the gateway.

Then the half-breed and the lawman drew their revolvers, Edge deliberately slowing himself to keep pace with the older but less experienced man at his side.

"No!" Patsy Blair shrieked.

"The double-crossing—" Logan started to rage.

"Ives?" Animal croaked.

"Assholes!" his partner forced around the constricting dread in his throat.

"Down!" Doyle roared.

Still half turned away from the front of the schoolhouse, Morrow and Edge leveled their revolvers across their bellies, right hands fisted to the butts as their left hands came across to fan the hammers. But as the lawman carried the action through to a conclusion, black powder smoke and flashes exploding from the muzzle of the big Walker Colt, the half-breed held back.

The Negro busied himself forward and down, arms spread wide to embrace all the children and bring them pitching to the ground with him. The screams of alarm vented by the small girls and the curses snarled by the boy were almost drowned by the barrage of gunfire from just one gun—until Morrow's six-shot revolver was emptied.

Spiro Logan and Patsy Blair were already silent and dropping to the ground before the children screamed. Had clutched at their heads as the sheriff opened fire and wrenched their suddenly bloody faces away from the blazing gun. They looked despairingly at the shocked Animal and Benedict Ives as they dropped to their knees and their bodies corkscrewed—the woman to turn over on to her back while the man went full length on his side, the both of them sprawled out across the corpses of Starky and the schoolteacher.

The half-breed's scowl was suddenly gone, replaced by an ice-cold grin that did not even hint at the exhilaration he felt within every part of his being as he squeezed the trigger of the Colt and began to fan the hammer, tracking the barrel to one side, then the other.

He blasted the first bullet into the chest of Benedict Ives, who already had his guns out of the holsters and cocked. And the man with the bushy mustache and buck teeth was able to get off a shot from each of his Colts as he was hit. But the bullets so fired burrowed harmlessly into the drying mud of the schoolyard several feet short of Edge and Morrow.

The second shot from the half-breed's gun took Animal in the fleshy chest, sent the ugly little man staggering back against the porch as he released the reins of two horses and clawed for his guns. He hit the wall and slid down it, his hands falling away from his holsters.

Edge shot Ives a second time then, in the belly, as the already wounded man hurled one gun away and used both hands to try to cock and aim the other one. Ives fell to his knees and sat back on his heels, resting the gun on the ground between his thighs.

The Frontier Colt tracked to Animal again as he was still sliding down the wall. Unable to tell if he was dead, Edge blasted a bullet into the top of his head; Animal's chin slumped forward and his hat slid off.

The horses that Animal had released as his last act in life wheeled and galloped across the schoolyard. The two still hitched to the other side of the porch were rearing and flailing their forelegs to tear themselves free of the tethers. Edge found himself momentarily distracted by the desperate efforts of the horses to get loose, but was nonetheless able to stay the movement of his gun as it swung to aim at Ives. The twice-shot man thrust his empty hands into the air in surrender.

But the Frontier Colt in the brown-skinned hand was still not empty. There remained two undischarged chambers in the cylinder of the revolver. And, although the half-breed's exhilaration at the success of his plan was no longer a factor in what he did, the killer's grin made him realize that his thirst for slaughter had not yet been fully satisfied.

Animal still twitched and jerked at the base of the schoolhouse wall beside the porch, writhing in his death throes. He spasmed twice more as the final bullets from the half-breed's gun impacted with his flesh.

The children were close to exhaustion and Doyle had little trouble in placating them as, in the wake of the two short bursts of gunfire, the advance of the people from town gradually, then more rapidly, quickened.

This as Edge and then Rich Morrow turned to start through the gateway and across the yard.

The lawman went forward with his big Walker Colt hanging down at his side in a loose grip. The half-breed thumbed aside the loading gate of his revolver to empty it of spent cartridges and then slid fresh rounds into the chambers. He did this blindly, with the skill of long experience, while he kept his eyes focused upon Benedict Ives.

The man who sat on his heels with his knees on the ground and his hands gradually sagging had a wound close to his heart and another in his belly, both blossoming large quantities of blood across his coat. But from the way he stared at the bloody heads of Spiro Logan and Patsy Blair it seemed he was more shocked by how they had been gunned down than by the way he had.

Only when Edge moved close to him did he at last drag his horrified gaze away to look elsewhere. And saw that the half-breed was unhitching the other two horses.

"Mostly I like most animals better than I like most humans, fellers," Edge said evenly. "Four-legged animals, you understand."

Ives, agony displacing shock on his face now, tried to talk, but failed.

Edge freed the horses and they wandered across to the other two in a far corner of the schoolyard. Then he told the pain-wracked man: "Sometimes I make an exception of kids like those you and your partners gave such a bad time to. Kids like that, they can be sort of like animals—helpless. And most times it isn't their

179

own fault they're where they're at. You okay, lady? Logan?''

There was no change of tone in the half-breed's voice. But he looked away from Benedict Ives and Ives peered in the same direction. And the pain on his buck-toothed, mustached face gave way to shock again—then incredulity, and finally a mixture of anger and despair as he accepted the proof before his eyes that he had been tricked. This as he saw the scowling Rich Morrow helping the bloody-faced woman and rancher to their feet.

"Had blanks in my gun, you murdering sonofabitch," the lawman explained bitterly. "The blood's from a fresh-stuck hog, sucker."

His bitterness was on the verge of turning to triumph. But Patsy Blair and Spiro Logan were too drained to express anything but exhaustion as they shook the empty bottles from their coat sleeves, then dropped the stoppers fixed with lengths of cord, which they had pulled out at the critical moment, drenching their heads with pig's blood when Morrow exploded the blanks.

"You assholes!" Ives managed to rasp through his prominent teeth now as Edge began to move back across the schoolyard, trailed by Logan, who had to help the woman; the both of them unsteady on their feet as they scrubbed at the drying animal blood on their faces and in their hair.

While he waited for Ives to breathe his last, Morrow retrieved the stolen bank money from the pockets of Animal's long coat.

By this time most of the Loganville citizenry that had rushed out to see the final violence at the schoolhouse had now started back toward Main Street. The freed children were at the center of the noisy, relieved group while near the back Olive Carlin was all but dragging her husband away from the temptation to offer solace to the distraught Widow Blair.

Edge recognized Abner Coburn and Joe Snyder among the group of mostly men who remained in front of the schoolyard gate. Doyle pointed out the grocer, Ben Wade, to him.

"You owe me change from ten bucks after the cost of two shots of rye," the half-breed said to the saloon keeper. Then, to the liveryman: "Left another ten spot at your place for boarding, feeding, watering, and currying my horse. Chestnut gelding in the stall—"

"It's this town owes you, seems to me, stranger," Coburn said. This produced a small chorus of sounds of agreement.

"I pay my own way and there's nothing owed," Edge answered evenly, taking out the makings from his shirt pocket. "Except by me to you, Wade."

"Huh?"

"Gave your wife a list of supplies. She didn't know the cost. Said the order'll be ready to pick up soon after nine tomorrow."

"Do my best," Wade answered.

"Obliged," Edge countered as most of those who had held back now started for town, escorting the rancher and the woman, who acknowledged Edge with curt nods but warmth in their eyes.

"You're leavin' tomorrow?" Doyle asked, watching eagerly for the half-breed to finish rolling the cigarette.

"Right."

Leaving the town most people were heading toward were the bearded Elmo Rankinn and his two sons. They reached the gateway at the same time as Rich Morrow.

"Okay for me and my boys to attend to the dead, Rich?" the undertaker asked.

Morrow, his hands filled with bills and a pocket of his pants bulged by chinking coins, growled: "Get right to it. The last one just died, dammit!"

The Rankinns moved off to collect up the bodies sprawled on the ground around the bullet-scarred entrance of the schoolhouse. And Ansel Twist captured the last of the four loose horses. For a moment, the lawman looked like he was going to say something to Edge, but he confined himself to a curt nod, as Patsy Blair and Spiro Logan had done. Except that there was resentment rather than warmth in his blue eyes as they briefly clashed with the glittering slits between the half breed's narrowed lids. Then he moved off toward Main Street with Glen Potts on one side and Ben Wade on the other.

"I'm not going to say that I'm not happy about having the kids safe and sound, of course," Morrow growled. "But I'm damn sure that if I'd been allowed to handle this thing my way from the start, the Rankinns wouldn't have so much work to do. And we'd have had those three bank-robbing killers in custody. To try and to hang by due process of Kansas justice. To let any other lawbreakers who might think they can come to Loganville know that they can't get away with . . ."

The sheriff's voice faded in the widening gap between him and his companions and Edge and Gideon Doyle.

"It was seein' the red ink on the hands of the Logan boy give you the idea, that right, mister?" the Negro asked.

"You got it, feller."

Doyle nodded and sighed. "Well, guess I'd better go show Betsy Blake her ever-lovin', no-account nigger come through this okay. Before I earn me a buck or two with some grave diggin'?"

"Suit yourself," Edge told him, and the black man finally acknowledged with a scowl that the half-breed was not going to pay him anything.

Then he directed his ill feeling toward the departing Morrow and sneered. "Somethin' else, mister. I reckon I know where you got the notion to use pig's blood from."

This drew no response from the white man, who was on the receiving end of another scowl as Doyle watched him push the makings back in a shirt pocket and light the cigarette angled from a side of his mouth. Until, once more, Gideon Doyle realized it would be more prudent to aim his displeasure at the absent sheriff. He spat and snarled: "That bastard Ives was right to call Morrow an asshole, I reckon." And now a mirthless grin showed more of his teeth. "On account of they say the law's an ass, ain't that right, mister?"

"Right," the half-breed replied evenly as he started back into the town he had reached just a few short hours but a lot of killings ago. "Though I don't know why they say that."

"You're kiddin' me, mister."

Edge showed him a glinting-eyed smile as he answered: "If the law's an ass, how come so many lawmen are so full of bullshit?"